VROOOMMM!

A NASComedy

by
Janet Allard

Conceived and developed with
Michael Bigelow Dixon

SAMUEL
FRENCH

FOUNDED 1830

NEW YORK HOLLYWOOD LONDON TORONTO

SAMUELFRENCH.COM

ISBN 978-0-573-66375-8   Printed in U.S.A.   #24647

IMPORTANT BILLING AND CREDIT REQUIREMENTS

VROOOMMM!

A NASComedy

By Janet Allard

Conceived and developed with Michael Bigelow Dixon

IMPORTANT NOTE TO LICENSEES

VROOOMMM! was commissioned with support from the Commonwealth Theatre Company's new play development program, Lanesboro, Minnesota. The play was also commissioned by Signature Theatre, Arlington, Virginia. It received developmental workshops at Commonweal Theatre Company, TheatreWorks in Palo Alto as part of their New Works Festival, 2005, The Playwrights' Center Playlabs Festival, and The Kennedy Center's Page-2-Stage Festival with Signature Theatre. *VROOOMMM!* received its first University production with the Carlton Players at Carleton College in 2005, directed by Liz Engelman.

VROOOMMM! was produced off Broadway as part of Arielle Tepper's Summer Play Festival in July 2007. The production was directed by David Lee; the set design was by Timothy Mackabee, the lighting design was by Dan Meeker, the costume design was by Caitlin Hunt, the sound design was by Sean Mahoney, the production stage manager was Naomi Anhorn, and the line producers were Caitlyn Thomson and Elin Eggertsdottir. The cast was as follows:

CHIP (also: **RANDY, JOANY**) . . . . Sarah Agnew

SLY (also: **RICHARD, CHICKEN 2, MITCHIE, WENDY**) . . Greer Goodman

HOTSHOT (also: **CHICKEN 1, MAN IN THE HAT, CASSIE,**
      NURSE) . . . . Meg Brogan

LEGS (also: **FLOSSIE, FLIP, FLASH**) . . . . Devon Berkshire

ROCKY (also: **WAITRESS, INSPECTOR**) . . . . Laura Jordan

RICHARD PETTY (also **NAKED FAN, SHADOWY FIGURE,**
      GRANDMA) . . . . Denise Lute

CHARACTERS

HOLLY "LEGS" NELSON: The only "woman" on the circuit. She's sexy, claims her femininity. #8 L'EGGS PANTYHOSE CHEVY.

KENNETH "ROCKY" KANE: The old pro. #47 COLONEL CLUCKER'S PONTIAC.

KENNY "HOTSHOT" KANE 3RD: Last season's Rookie of the Year. Rocky's son. He's the guy to beat. #7 BIG RED GUM FORD.

CHIP "CHIP" CHOWALSKY: 30's. A driver with some really bad luck. #13 LUCKY CHARMS DODGE.

CHARLIE "SLY" FOX: A mysterious "man" in mirrored sunglasses and flashy clothes. #24 VICTORIA'S SECRET DODGE.

FLIP: A race fan. Dad.

JOANY: A race fan. Mom.

CASSIE: A race fan. Their teenage daughter.

MITCHIE: Their teenage son. Not a race fan.

GRANDMA: Asleep at the track.

A NAKED FAN: A genuine dedicated all-American NASCAR fan.

THE INSPECTOR: The official NASCAR inspector. A cross between Doctor Ruth and Peter Lorre.

THE MAN IN THE HAT: A good 'ol boy. He owns NASCAR.

CHICKEN #1: The Official Mascot of Colonel Clucker's Chicken. A sponsor.

THE NURSE: The official Nurse of NASCAR.

CHICKEN #2: Same suit, different person.

FLOSSIE: Rocky's dead wife.

THE WAITRESS: Just a waitress.

RANDY "STONEWALL" JACKSON: An Announcer. From the South. Very Good Ol' Boy.

RICHARD HARDEN: An Announcer. From the North. Very Ivy League.

RICHARD PETTY: The king of racing.

SETTING

On the NASCAR racing circuit.

TIME

Now.

CASTING

(all characters played by women)

Actor # 1: **CHIP, RANDY, JOANY.**
Actor # 2: **LEGS, FLOSSIE, FLIP, FLASH**
Actor # 3: **SLY, RICHARD, CHICKEN 2, MITCHIE, WENDY**
Actor # 4: **ROCKY, WAITRESS, INSPECTOR**
Actor # 5: **HOTSHOT, CHICKEN 1, MAN IN THE HAT, CASSIE, NURSE**
Actor # 6: **RICHARD PETTY, NAKED FAN, SHADOWY FIGURE, GRANDMA**

	Actor #1	Actor #2	Actor #3	Actor #4	Actor #5	Actor#6
Drivers:	**CHIP**	**LEGS**	**SLY**	**ROCKY**	**HOTSHOT**	
Announcers:	**RANDY**		**RICHARD**			
Other:	**FLOSSIE**	**CHICKEN 2**	**WAITRESS**	**CHICKEN 1**		**RICHARD PETTY**
					NURSE	**NAKED FAN**
						SHADOWY
						FIGURE
Inspection:			**INSPECTOR**	**MAN IN**		
Fan Family:	**JOANY**	**FLIP**	**MITCHIE**	**THE HAT**	**CASSIE**	**GRANDMA**
Drivers in Disguise:		**FLASH**	**WENDY**			

NOTE: The casting of Richard and Randy depends on how they will be presented. This script is written for Richard to be played Actor #3, and Randy to be played by Actor #1 (Randy). For the Playlabs workshop, however, all of the actors played Randy and Richard (switching off for different scenes). Or, Richard and Randy can appear on video, audio or can be done with cardboard cutouts, action figures or faces on Popsicle sticks – or any other theatrical convention which allows the actors to switch in and out of these characters instantaneously.

NOTE #2: The program for this production should list Actor #6 only as "Grandma," or "Special Guest Star." Richard Petty and the Naked Fan should be a surprise for the audience.

THE DESIGN

For the off-off Broadway production, a bare stage and several set elements were used to create the many different locations of the NASCAR world.

The races were choreographed in rolling chairs color-coordinated to match the suits of the racers. Sound and lighting effects helped create the world of the race.

For the Karaoke Bar, checkerboard-toped tables on casters rolled in, the rolling "racing chairs" became seats at the bar tables, the announcer's booth on wheels spun around to become the bar and a microphone and some mood lighting completed the Karaoke Bar atmosphere.

The Garage was created by pushing together several chairs to create the idea of a race-car. The bar on wheels became part of the Garage architecture. The locker room consisted of a bench and some lockers on wheels.

A bench placed downstage became the race-way stands for the fan scene and also the scene with Rocky and Flash.

The actors remained in their racing-suits throughout the entire show and costume pieces were added over or under the race-suits for character changes. Hats, sunglasses, wigs, etc. were effective ways of defining a new character while allowing for a quick transformation.

Part of the joy of this play for the audience is watching the 5 actresses transform from one character to another – watching the space morph from race-track to Karaoke Bar in the blink of an eye. These transitions were exposed, rather than hidden from the audience.

THE MUSIC

Rights to produce this play do not include rights to use the music referred to in the play.

The lyrics in the play are original and may either be sung to Karaoke tracks of existing songs if rights are obtained, or you may choose to compose your own original Karaoke music.

SCENE ONE: Welcome Race Fans

(A sound montage. In the dark, over the loudspeakers we hear the deafening sound of stock car engines starting up. A snippet of the American Anthem, F-16 fighter jets fly overhead. A voice [maybe the President, maybe Richard Petty] says: Gentlemen, start your engines." The lights rise on the 5 **RACERS** *decked out in racing suits. They stand in front of colorful rolling chairs – their "stock cars," facing the audience. The following lines are divided amongst the cast.)*

RACERS.

Welcome, Race Fans!

This is Daytona Baby!

The monster track that snacks on Pontiacs

120 laps to go –

Calamity in turn four.

Chaos in turn two

(The **RACERS** *slide into their stock-car chairs.)*

100

90

80

70

50 laps to go!

(The **RACERS** *in line, weave high and low on the track.)*

four tires

two tires

two tires

four tires, just gas

just gas

goin' into pit road
coming out of pit road
4th
5th
6th
7th caution of the day!
tight
loose
loose
tight
yellow flag
green flag
yellow flag
green flag
yellow
green
yellow
green, green green green!

(They all turn, putting the petal to the floorboard, leaning back in the driver's seat:)

10
9
8
7
6
5 Laps to go!

(The sound of stock car engines. **ACTOR #1** *and* **ACTOR #3** *peel off US to change to* **RICHARD** *and* **RANDY** *while* **ROCKY**, **HOTSHOT**, *and* **LEGS** *race in line, facing audience.)*

HOTSHOT, ROCKY & LEGS. Wooooweee!!

ROCKY. Come on, Son! Just try to catch your old man! I may be old but I'm not slow.

HOTSHOT. I'm on your tail old man!

ROCKY. Woowee!

*(All **RACERS** turn up stage as **ACTOR #1** and **ACTOR #3** appear in the announcer's booth as **RICHARD** and **RANDY** on the air.)*

RICHARD. 5 Laps to go! Randy, this has been a monumentally exciting race at the Daytona Crunch-n-Munch 500.

RANDY. A Knucklebiter from start to finish!

RICHARD. And it is not over –

RANDY. Till the fat lady sings.

RICHARD. Until the checkered flag is waved. Florida doesn't get any hotter than this.

RANDY. Actually, Rich, it does. When I was drivin' this track in the Spit-n-Chew Tobacco 500 in '89 it was so hot in that driver's seat my butt blistered up –

RICHARD. You're a real trooper, Randy.

RANDY. Let me tell you Richey, we didn't have newfangled cooling hoses back then, we had to suck on an ice cube to get us through –

RICHARD	**RANDY.**
And #36 loses control	WHOA BABY!
#36 into the wall	Here it comes, here it comes!
4 is on top of 36, 18 is in it	Holy Moley Toledo
29, 18, 34, 38, 32 all in it	I can't believe my eyes
Here comes the caution flag	Jiminy Christmas what a doozy
And the caution's out, caution's out	Caution flag. Caution flag.

(They emerge from behind the booth, coming downstage to take a look at the catastrophe.)

RANDY. I told him not to bring his dog into the pit with him. I don't know what he's gonna do for hunting. Dog parts everywhere. It reminds me of my dog, Richey – Little Cupcake –

RICHARD. We'd like to take this brief opportunity to thank our sponsors.

RANDY. Special Thanks to BooHoo's Butt Paste, Udder Balm Teat Grease, Bubba's Double Bubble Yum Gum, Pampers for Grampers, Papa's Popular Pork Rinds and Colonel Cluckers Chicken, it's "Slap your Mama" Good.

RICHARD. Not to forget, Mrs. Moody's Moonshine Moon Pies.

RANDY. They're Mmm good. In case you haven't noticed, this is Randy "Stonewall" Jackson on the Right-

RICHARD. And Richard Harden –

RANDY. Hard on?

RICHARD. Harden. On the Left.

RANDY. Welcome to RACING, Dick!

RICHARD. Actually, I prefer Richard, Randy, I'm –

RANDY. You look like a poodle dressed up for a parade, Dickey. You better get you some new racing duds, Bubba!

RICHARD. I believe that's the green flag, Randy –

RANDY. Well, Slap my Mama! Green Green Green, Boogidy Boogidy Boogidy! Get it on Boys!

(**RACERS** *all turn to SR.*)

RICHARD. And woman. There's a woman.

(**RACERS** *turn to face DS.*)

RANDY. A woman?

(**RACERS** *turn to SL.*)

RICHARD & RANDY. Where'd she come from?

(*Loud engine sounds. Race cars roaring – as the* **RACERS** *face the audience. Driving. Hectic. End of a race.*)

LEGS. Hi Boys.

ALL. Where'd she come from?

LEGS. I got the horsepower today, fellas!

ROCKY. Get back in it!

(**RACERS** *slide into a line facing SL.*)

HOTSHOT. Get off my tail, Lady.

LEGS. I got a bumper and I'm not afraid to use it.

SLY. I'm too loose.

HOTSHOT. I'm tight in the turns.

CHIP. I'm Juuuuuuust right!

ROCKY. Win or die tryin'.

SLY. Easy does it.

ROCKY. First or fighting!

CHIP. Today's my day!!! Praise Elvis!

(*LOUD SOUND*)

What was that?

ROCKY. Whoa! Something's not right. Stay with me, Flossie!

CHIP. Where are my tires!? They come right off it! Did ya tighten my nuts, boys?

(**CHIP** *spirals out of control. The actor playing* **CHIP** *transitions to* **RANDY**.)

ROCKY. I'm not outta gas! Am I boys? Shit, I'm outta gas.

(**ROCKY** *putters out.*)

HOTSHOT. Show me what you got, girl.

LEGS. I'm going high.

SLY. Go high, go high.

LEGS. I got him.

SLY. We got him.

LEGS. Slingshot!

(**LEGS** *and* **SLY** *slingshot past* **HOTSHOT**.)

SLY. Weeeeeeeooooooooooooo!

(**SLY** *spins out to transition into* **RICHARD**.)

LEGS. Wooooooooweeeeeeeeee!

HOTSHOT. Will you look at that.

(*Lights down on the* **RACERS** *and up on* **RICHARD** *and* **RANDY** *in the announcer's booth.*)

RANDY. What the holey heck?

RICHARD. And Holly "Legs" Nelson –

RANDY. She's stealing it away from you boys!

RICHARD. Crosses the line to –

RANDY. Steal the checkers right out from under 'um!

RICHARD. To win her first race ever here –

RANDY. Where in the wonderful world, Richey, did she come out of? You got to ask yourself –

RICHARD. Making racing history here at Daytona –

RANDY. They didn't have Legs Pantyhose cars in my day –

RICHARD. As she heads to Victory Lane.

(The sound of cheering as we transition to the locker room.)

SCENE TWO: Sore Losers

(Lockers and a bench. And Beer. After a race. The four **RACERS** *stand, totally dismayed. They discuss.)*

ROCKY. Sure is amazing, Hotshot, a woman like that, beating you.

(pause)

SLY. Sure is.

ROCKY. Sure is incredible.

CHIP. Sure is miraculous.

HOTSHOT. Come on Chip.

CHIP. She sure got good fuel mileage.

ROCKY. INCREDIBLE fuel mileage.

SLY. MIRACULOUS fuel mileage.

HOTSHOT. Oh, come on.

SLY. I bet you a million dollars she's not running legal.

HOTSHOT. Get outta here, Sly.

SLY. Word gets around.

CHIP. Word does.

ROCKY. Heard her mechanics braggin' in the bar.

CHIP. What's the scuttlebutt?

ROCKY. I hear she's got soft tires.

SLY. She soaks her tires with that tire softening soaker.

ROCKY. I hear she dropped a load of buckshot on the track, made her car 300 lbs. lighter.

HOTSHOT. Nah.

SLY. Heard her helmet was made outta lead.

CHIP. Yep. She passed it out the window on the 1st stop.

SLY. Made her car 50 lbs. lighter.

HOTSHOT. So she got some good gas mileage –

SLY. INCREDIBLE gas mileage.

ROCKY. MIRACULOUS gas mileage.

SLY. I hear she's got an extra fuel tank hidden up in there somewhere.

ROCKY. I hear they found fuel additive in her catch man's catch can.

CHIP. Truth is they caught her with a screwy rear fascia.

HOTSHOT. Nah, she replaced the offensive rear fascia.

CHIP. But she replaced the one she replaced with another screwy rear fascia.

ALL. *(but* **HOTSHOT***)* OH.

HOTSHOT. Huh.

SLY. Just like a woman. To cheat.

CHIP. I would never cheat.

ROCKY. Me neither.

HOTSHOT. That's right, Daddy.

ROCKY. No cheatin'.

ALL. *(but* **HOTSHOT***)* No way.

ROCKY. Wouldn't be fair to you boys.

SLY. Don't need to cheat when you win anyway.

  (pause)

HOTSHOT. I hear you've got an illegal restrictor plate, Sly.

SLY. Rocky, I hear you rig your bumper to fall off.

ROCKY. I hear you've got a wedge in there, Chip, that comes out and drops your car 4 inches.

CHIP. I hear you've got an oversized engine, Hotshot.

HOTSHOT. The point is, the rulebook is like the Bible, boys –

ALL. Open to interpretation.

ROCKY. It's one thing to find the "grey areas" of the rule book.

SLY. It's one thing to push the envelope.

ROCKY. It's one thing to seek the "competitive advantage."

CHIP. To fudge an inch here or a ½ inch there.

ALL. *(but* **HOTSHOT***)* IT'S ANOTHER THING TO CHEAT.

SLY. Can't let her get away with that.

ROCKY. They should take away her win.

CHIP. Send her to the room of doom.

ALL. Hang her out to dry.

> *(All but* **ROCKY** *and* **HOTSHOT** *exit.* **ROCKY** *looks at his son.)*

ROCKY. Sure is amazing, Son. A woman like that, beating you.

HOTSHOT. Huh.

> *(Lights out on the locker room as we transition to* **RICH-ARD** *and* **RANDY** *mid-broadcast.)*

SCENE THREE: Is That a Sport?

(**RICHARD** *and* **RANDY** *on the air.*)

RICHARD. And that's the #7 Big Red Gum Ford avoiding the accident.

RANDY. Skating through that rats nest free and clear, Bubba!

RICHARD. Well driven!

RANDY. Well driven?

RICHARD. That is a marvelous example of automotive execution there by Kenny Hotshot Kane the 3rd, here at the Darlington double-wide double-dipped, Duncan Doughnuts, mmmm delectable Superspeedway.

RANDY. This track'll eatcher ass.

RICHARD. Colorful image, Randy.

RANDY. Pull my finger.

RICHARD. What?

RANDY. Tell the folks where you're from, Dickey.

RICHARD. Originally I hail from New England where I –

RANDY. Didn't you just cover the ladies swimsuit competition at Well-Lezzy?

RICHARD. Actually, it was the Women's Water Ballet at Wellesley.

RANDY. Is that a sport?

RICHARD. And we're just about ready to proceed here.

RANDY. GREEN GREEN GREEN! Boogidy boogidy boogidy!

RICHARD. There they go.

RANDY. And here they come – Hotshot Big Red Gum leading the pack –

RICHARD. With L'eggs Pantyhose creeping up! –

RANDY. And Kenny Hotshot Kane pulling away with just a lap to go!

Last year's Rookie of the year, back on track! Woooooowwwwweeeeee –

(*LOUD ENGINE SOUNDS. REALLY LOUD. DEAF-ENING.*)

SCENE FOUR: Hide and Seek

(Outside the garage. A trash can on stage. **HOTSHOT**
enters. Looks around. Acting suspicious. Approaches the
trash can. **ROCKY** *enters behind him.)*

ROCKY. How's inspection goin', son?

HOTSHOT. Just about done.

ROCKY. What're you doing out here?

HOTSHOT. Stepped out for a smoke.

ROCKY. Can I bum one?

HOTSHOT. Must've left um inside. I'll go get um.

ROCKY. They find anything unusual?

HOTSHOT. Nothing illegal.

ROCKY. Good for you. Celebrate at the bar?

HOTSHOT. In a minute, Daddy. I'll meetcha.

*(***ROCKY*** exits.)*

*(***HOTSHOT*** drops a metal object into the trash can.*
Exits.)

*(***CHIP*** slinks in, reaches into the trash can.* **SLY** *comes in*
behind him.)

SLY. Hey Chip, whatcha doin' in the trash?

CHIP. Looking –

Looking for my –

Hotdog.

*(***CHIP*** pulls hotdog out of trash can.)*

Dropped it.

Found it.

Mmmmm.

SLY. You gonna eat that?

CHIP. Last bite's the best bite. Want it? You want it, don't
ya?

SLY. Nah, you go ahead.

CHIP. Mmmmmmm.

(choke)

SLY. You better get a drink. Wash that down.

(CHIP gives SLY the thumbs up, exits, choking. SLY goes to trash can, looks in. Holds up a piece of metal, examines it. LEGS enters.)

LEGS. Oh, good.

SLY. Oh, Legs!

LEGS. You found it. Thanks. I've been looking for that.

SLY. What is it?

LEGS. Oh Sly, I think you know what that is.
Give it here.

SLY. You don't expect me to give this up for nothing, do you?

LEGS. You wouldn't hold out on a girl.

SLY. Finders keepers.

LEGS. Name your price.

(HOTSHOT enters.)

HOTSHOT. What are you doing with that?

SLY. It's mine.

HOTSHOT. It's yours? It's illegal.

SLY. It's hers.

LEGS. No it's not.

HOTSHOT. Give it to me, I'll get rid of it.

LEGS. Give it to me, I don't trust him.

SLY. What is it?

HOTSHOT. *(to LEGS)* What is it?

LEGS. What does it look like?

SLY. A slinky?

HOTSHOT & LEGS. That's right.

SLY. Shit, I could buy one of those at Toys R US. See you guys at the bar.

(SLY gives it to LEGS and exits.)

HOTSHOT. Give it back.

LEGS. You don't expect me to give this up for nothing, do you?

HOTSHOT. You wouldn't hold out on a guy.

LEGS. Finders keepers.

HOTSHOT. Name your price.

LEGS. What can you give me I haven't already got?

HOTSHOT. A date to the prom.

LEGS. Sorry, I don't mix business with pleasure.

HOTSHOT. Just thought you might want to get your mind off your business.

LEGS. I'm all business till I beat you again.

HOTSHOT. That's too bad, cuz I'm a good kisser.

LEGS. Good, then you can practice on my rear fascia. See you on the track.

(Racing sounds as we transition to **RICHARD** *and* **RANDY** *on the air.)*

RANDY. Last lap here at Martinsville Monster Speedway: The Paper Clip of Philadelphia –

RICHARD. And L'eggs Pantyhose, coming from the back of the pack SPRINGS into first place!

(sound: BOING!)

RANDY. Jumpin' baby Jehosephat on a pogo stick, I have never seen anything like that. What's she got in that engine? A bungee cord?

RICHARD. A mighty well-deserved victory, here at –

RANDY. Shut-up Dick.

SCENE FIVE: A Friendly Wager

(Karaoke music plays as we transition to the Karaoke Bar: "THE THIRSTY WORM." A bar with stools and a table with chairs. A neon sign or two. After the race. **LEGS** *sings QUEEN OF THE ROAD her victory Karaoke song.* **SLY** *and* **CHIP** *drown their sorrows [singing back-up].* **ROCKY** *sits and watches.)*

LEGS. Welcome, everybody to Karaoke Wednesdays here at the Thirsty Worm in Paperclip, Philadelphia. I'm miss Holly "Legs" Nelson, and in case you Dingleberries weren't watching live at home on the Speed Network (channel 2,075). Me and my Pantyhose Chevy kicked just a little bit of ass out there on the track today. So raise your PBR's and your Smirnoff Ice and let's celebrate. This one goes out to Kenny "buckshot," I mean…Hotshot…Kane.

*(**HOTSHOT** enters unseen and stands in the corner watching her sing.)*

QUEEN OF THE ROAD (Based on King of the Road by Roger Miller)

LEGS.

    CHECKERED FLAG, AND VICTORY LANE!
    POP THE CORK OFF MY CHAMPAGNE!
    NO FROWNS, NO TEARS, REGRETS…

ROCKY. I'm goin' out for cigarettes.

LEGS.

    AH BUT, TWO HOURS OF LEADING THE PACK, LEFT
    YOUR SORRY ASSES WAY IN BACK.
    I'M NOT YOUR KING BY NO MEANS, I'M
    QUEEN OF THE ROAD.

CHIP & SLY.

    L'EGGS PANTYHOSE ON THE CLIMB
    KANE DYNASTY LEFT BEHIND

LEGS.

    I'LL TEACH YA HOW TO MAKE A BUCK…

    *(**HOTSHOT** interrupts.)*

HOTSHOT. What the fuck are you boys doing?

(*Music out.*)

CHIP. DOGHOUSE Lady.

SLY. You put us in the DOGHOUSE!

HOTSHOT. (*to* **LEGS**) You pass inspection?

LEGS. Flying colors.

HOTSHOT. Alright, I'm making a bet.

ROCKY. Are we bettin'?

CHIP. Well all right! A little money on the side!

HOTSHOT. Ante up, boys. The lady's won two. Beginners luck. Fifty bucks says she can't win a third.

LEGS. Only fifty?

HOTSHOT. A hundred.

SLY. A hundred it is. I'll put my money on the Lady.

CHIP. Whoa! Me too.

HOTSHOT. Daddy?

(*pause*)

Daddy.

ROCKY. Well, I'm can't bet against my own son.

HOTSHOT. Thanks old man.

ROCKY. Unless. What odds you giving?

LEGS. You fellas are making me blush.

CHIP. Wait a minute. What if one of us wins?

LEGS. Winner takes all.

ALL. Winner takes all.

HOTSHOT. And no cheating.

ALL. And no cheating.

HOTSHOT. I'll hold the money.

(**HOTSHOT** *takes the money and exits.* **CHIP** *slides up to* **LEGS**, *engaging her in conversation.*)

CHIP. You know, I'm thinking I got to get a new racing technique. Something to change my luck. Got any ideas?

LEGS. Why don't you paint your car a different color?

ROCKY. Yeah, pink.

CHIP. You think that'll help get me in touch with my feminine side?

(The guys laugh.)

CHIP. What? What's wrong with getting in touch with your feminine side?

ROCKY. You already look like a girl with that ponytail.

CHIP. Cut off the mullet?! This thing is a chick magnet. Business in the front, party in the back. Right? Am I right?

LEGS. Maybe you've got a voodoo hex on you.

ROCKY. Maybe you should go to church and pray.

CHIP. I got Jesus and Buddha and Vishnu and Shiva and Elvis hanging from the dashboard. I got a Confucius on order.

ROCKY. You got too many of them. They're confused. I'm goin' out to the Pump and Munch for some smokes. See you boys later.

*(**ROCKY** exits.)*

SLY. Maybe you should make things right with those exwives of yours.

*(**CHIP** considers.)*

CHIP. Nah. I want to do a song.

(yelling to the waitress to put on a Karaoke track)

Number 69, Sylvia!

SLY. Want to dance, Lady?

LEGS. All right.

*(**CHIP** sings RICHARD PETTY, karaoke style. **SLY** and **LEGS** do the back-up karaoke dance moves joining in to sing the chorus.)*

RICHARD PETTY (based on the 60's hit RUNNING BEAR by JP Richardson)

1ST VERSE:

IN THE STANDS OF DAYTONA, STOOD RICHARD
PETTY, YOUNG RACER BRAVE.
ON THE OTHER SIDE OF THE TRACK
STOOD A LOVELY NASCAR MAID.
DIXIE WHITE TRASH WAS HER NAME,
SUCH A LOVELY SIGHT TO SEE
BUT HER DAD WAS AN EARNHARDT FAN,
SO THEIR LOVE COULD NEVER BE.

CHORUS:

OH, RICHARD PETTY LOVES DIXIE WHITE TRASH,
WITH A LOVE BIG AS THE SKY.
OH, RICHARD PETTY LOVES DIXIE WHITE TRASH,
WITH A LOVE THAT HE CAN'T HIDE.

2ND VERSE:

THEY COULDN'T CROSS THE BURNING BLACKTOP,
BECAUSE THE BLACKTOP WAS TOO WIDE.
HE COULDN'T REACH HIS DIXIE WHITE TRASH
WAITING ON THE OTHER SIDE.
IN THE MOONLIGHT HE COULD SEE HER,
THROWING BEER CANS IN THE STANDS.
HER LITTLE HEART WAS BEATING FASTER, WAITING
FOR HER RACIN' MAN.

CHORUS:

OH, RICHARD PETTY LOVES DIXIE WHITE TRASH,
WITH A LOVE BIG AS THE SKY.
OH, RICHARD PETTY LOVES DIXIE WHITE TRASH,
WITH A LOVE THAT HE CAN'T HIDE.

3RD VERSE:

RICHARD PETTY JUMPED ON THE RACE TRACK
DIXIE WHITE TRASH DID THE SAME
AS THEY SPRINTED TOWARDS EACH OTHER
ROUND THE CORNER THE CARS CAME
AS THEIR HANDS TOUCHED AND THEIR LIPS MET
THE STOCK CAR ENGINES ROARED THEM DOWN

NOW THEY'LL ALWAYS BE TOGETHER IN THAT HAPPY
HUNTING GROUND.

CHORUS:
OH, RICHARD PETTY LOVES DIXIE WHITE TRASH,
WITH A LOVE BIG AS THE SKY.
OH, RICHARD PETTY LOVES DIXIE WHITE TRASH,
WITH A LOVE THAT HE CAN'T HIDE.

Karaoke Koreography:

Oh: *hands in 'O' over head*

Richard Petty: *Finger on the upper lip to indicate mustache.*

Loves: *hug yourself*

Dixie White Trash: *one hand on hip, one behind head (glamour pose)*

Big as the sky: *raise arms overhead and open in arc to sides*

He can't hide: *hands covering private parts*

Track: *motions with hands*

Lovely NASCAR Maid: *Hands supporting big breasts.*

Sight to see: *point to eyes*

Dad was an Earnhardt fan: *3 fingers to indicate the #3*

Never be: *head and finger shaking no*

SCENE SIX: Seductive Chicken

(As **CHIP** *sings the final chorus,* **SLY** *and* **LEGS** *dance offstage together leaving* **CHIP** *alone to sing his heart out, doing some sexy dance moves.)*

(Someone in a chicken suit steps out of the shadows. We can see the actor's face in the chicken costume. That's part of the fun. This is **CHICKEN 1**.*)*

CHICKEN 1. Psst.

Psssssssssst.

Chowalsky!

CHIP. What the –

CHICKEN 1. Shhhh.

CHIP. Colonel Cluckers Chicken! I LOVE YOU!

CHICKEN 1. Shhhh.

CHIP. I love your chicken. If you're looking for Rocky –

CHICKEN 1. I'm not looking for Rocky, I'm looking for you.

CHIP. Man, COLONEL CLUCKERS! You're REAL chicken! You are the best!

(The **CHICKEN** *offers him a piece out of a big bucket of chicken.)*

CHICKEN 1. Chicken? Go ahead, have a thigh.

CHIP. I'm a breast man, myself. Ummm. Those spices!

CHICKEN 1. I'm a fan of yours too, Chowalsky. We've got something to "discuss." A proposition.

CHIP. Have I told you, I love your skin.

CHICKEN 1. We're a perfect match, wouldn't you say?

I mean your face screams "Chicken."

CHIP. What are you saying?

CHICKEN 1. Your personality promotes poultry.

CHIP. Wait a minute, you're not looking for a new driver, are you?

CHICKEN 1. Not officially, Chip.

CHIP. I mean, you're still with Kane Racing right? Rocky Kane and Colonel Cluckers are –

CHICKEN 1. Hand in glove. But if we were looking –

CHIP. But you're not.

CHICKEN 1. Not officially, but if we were –

CHIP. But why would you be –

CHICKEN 1. We'd be looking for you.

CHIP. But I'm a loser. My tires fell off today –

CHICKEN 1. There are Has-beens and there are Yet-to-be's.

CHIP. My engine burst into flames last week – I'm snake-bit, I've got a stroke of bad luck I just can't shake.

CHICKEN 1. Well, if you're not interested – I can take my chicken elsewhere –

CHIP. Wait. Colonel Cluckers wants me?

CHICKEN 1. You drive chicken, walk chicken, talk chicken, sing chicken, make folks think, feel, live and breathe chicken!

CHIP. I just got a call from Preparation H this morning. I'm sitting on their offer.

CHICKEN 1. Well, sit on us. Unless you're not interested in promoting perfect poultry.

CHIP. This conversation is making me uncomfortable.

CHICKEN 1. What conversation?

We're not having a conversation.

CHIP. What about Rocky? What's happening to Rocky?

CHICKEN 1. Sleep on it.

CHICKEN 1. And Pal,

You never saw me.

(The **CHICKEN** *exits.)*

CHIP. Fucking chicken.

(Lights down as we transition to:)

SCENE SEVEN: Favors. In the Bar

(A Karaoke bar that looks exactly like the one in the previous scene. Only we're in another town on the race circuit. In this bar, a neon sign reads "THE THIRSTY ARMADILLO." ROCKY, a beer in each hand steps up to the Karaoke microphone. A song starts – reminiscent of a karaoke version of Patsy Klein's "After Midnight.")

ROCKY. Welcome to Thirsty Thursday's at the Thirsty Armadillo in Badax, Michigan. This one goes out to Flossie.

(sings)

I GO OUT DRIVING AFTER MIDNIGHT
UNDER THE MOONLIGHT
DOWN ACROSS THE SILVER SANDS
I GO OUT DRIVING RUNNING MOONSHINE
AND LOOKIN FOR YOU.

(As he sings, a shadowy woman enters. She wears a big black sunhat with a veil covering her face. A sexy ghost. This is FLOSSIE. She leans against the bar. ROCKY sits – 2 beers in hand. As the music plays on:)

ROCKY. Well here we are again Flossie, same bar different town, different town, same bar.
And Colonel Clucker doesn't return my calls.
God Damn chicken.
You think there's some funny business going on?
Ah, you're right, I'm just being paranoid.
How bout you? How are things goin'? Happy?
Hotshot's doing well, ya know, but he's got a head the size of a hot air balloon.
You think he got that from me, huh? Go ahead, you can say it.
You think I should take up Paraskiing?
Or Alpine peak jumping?
Yeah, you're right. There's time for everything. I'm not that old.
Am I old, Flossie?
Ahh, listen to me.

(FLOSSIE starts to leave.)

ROCKY. You want to dance, Flossie?

(She stands in the doorway, watching him.)

Nah, you're right. That would be creepy and weird.

(She exits.)

Hey, you left your beer here, you mind if I?

(But she's gone.)

Yeah, okay, I'll just finish it for you.

(HOTSHOT enters.)

HOTSHOT. Who you talking to, old man?

ROCKY. Nobody. Darts?

HOTSHOT. Not after last time.

ROCKY. Come on.

HOTSHOT. No losing your temper.

ROCKY. No leaning in over the line.

(HOTSHOT takes out his darts. Bar music plays. A father and son song.)

HOTSHOT. You hear from the Chicken lately?

(He throws.)

ROCKY. Why?

HOTSHOT. Just curious.

(He throws.)

ROCKY. Is there something to hear?

HOTSHOT. Nah. I don't know. Rumors.

(He throws.)

ROCKY. You ever think about if it comes down to me and you?

HOTSHOT. What?

(Hotshot collects the darts, gives them to Rocky.)

ROCKY. Way out in front of the pack. Just us two.

HOTSHOT. What are you saying, Daddy?

ROCKY. I'm saying, Kenneth, if it comes down to me and you –

(He throws.)

HOTSHOT. Me and you, what?

ROCKY. Leading the pack.

(He throws.)

HOTSHOT. We race. Right? What are you saying?

ROCKY. We race.

(He throws.)

HOTSHOT. Are you asking me – what are you asking?

ROCKY. *(Collecting the darts.)* If it comes down to just me and you – a guy needs a win, you know, you go too long without a win and people start to think you don't have it in you, you know –

HOTSHOT. I wouldn't let you win.

ROCKY. I'm not asking you –

HOTSHOT. Well, good.

(Hotshot throws.)

ROCKY. I'm not asking you to cheat – just if it came down to the two of us, and your choice was to -

HOTSHOT. Win or not win?

(Hotshot throws.)

I'd win.

(Hotshot throws.)

ROCKY. *(Rocky collects the darts.)* I'm just saying, there's a thing called teamwork. There's a way of working together, you help me out, I help you out.

HOTSHOT. I wouldn't give it to you. I wouldn't insult you.

ROCKY. Give it to me. Now you're getting cocky.

(Rocky takes aim.)

HOTSHOT. You're over the line.

ROCKY. I'm on the line.

HOTSHOT. Your toes are over.

ROCKY. You start getting cocky, you start to have to live up to your own mouth –

HOTSHOT. Race the track, not the racer, isn't that what you say?

ROCKY. Give it 20 years, you'll know what that's like. I wasn't over.

(Rocky throws.)

HOTSHOT. You're not dead yet, old man.

ROCKY. Who said I was dead –

*(**HOTSHOT** pulls out his money to pay for the drinks.)*

HOTSHOT. I'm not going to let you win.

ROCKY. Just don't let it devastate you. Don't let it kill ya, when I take the title right out from under you. When, your own flesh and blood steals it away. Don't let it get to you.

HOTSHOT. When it comes down to me and you, I don't care who you are, I'm gonna kick your ass.

ROCKY. Unless I kick yours first.

HOTSHOT. Cheers.

*(**HOTSHOT** puts his money on the bar.)*

ROCKY. No, I got this, it's on me, Son.

HOTSHOT. No, here.

ROCKY. What did I tell you? I got it.

HOTSHOT. Sure.

*(**HOTSHOT** walks away. **ROCKY** looks in his wallet. It's empty.)*

ROCKY. Shit.

*(**ROCKY** exits.)*

SCENE EIGHT: Mystery Man

(Same bar. At a table. **SLY** *builds a house out of cards.* **CHIP** *enters. Music plays in the background. A love song.)*

CHIP. So, what happened to you last night?
Last I knew you were closing down the bar again with Miss Holly Nelson.
So what happened?

*(***SLY*** *is silent. He builds.)*

CHIP. Man, how do you do it? You're the talk of the track. What's Sly up to? Where's Sly tonight? How come he spends so much time in that tinted up trailer of his?

SLY. Shhhhh.

CHIP. You know I got looks, I got charm, I got the sunglasses, got the hair, got it all man.
What have you got that I don't got?

*(***SLY*** *shrugs.)*

SLY. Keep it low, man.

CHIP. What do you mean, like talk low, like really deep, like "Hey Baby I'm your Barry White."

SLY. No. Keep it quiet man.

CHIP. Quiet.

SLY. Yeah, just keep it down. You're gonna give me a reputation.

CHIP. I wish I had your reputation. You know I keep trying to figure out what I do wrong.

SLY. Get a new mechanic.

CHIP. Not with the car, with the ladies. I mean you'd think being married 4 times I would've gotten it at least ¼ right half the time.

*(***SLY*** *shrugs.* **WAITRESS** *enters humming a song – the same tune* **ROCKY** *sang in the last scene – different lyrics.)*

WAITRESS.

> I GO OUT DRIVIN'
> WITH MY BOYFRIEND
> OUT IN THE MOONLIGHT
> IN HIS BIG OL' NASCAR CAR
> *(She hums the rest.)*
>
> *(They watch her. Appreciating her beauty.)*

CHIP. Good thing there are always more fish in the sea.

> *(**SLY** raises his glass.)*

You want another? On me, what are you drinking?

SLY. Cranberry.

CHIP. Cranberry? And what?

SLY. Cranberry spritzer.

CHIP. Cranberry spritzer, Sylvia. Two.

> *(The **WAITRESS** flirts with **SLY**, ignores **CHIP**.)*

WAITRESS. Hi Sly. How ya doin?

CHIP. Hi Sylvia.

WAITRESS. That was some kinda race last night. I was watching your every move.

CHIP. Hi Sylvia.

WAITRESS. You were weaving in and out and in and out of traffic –

CHIP. Hello Sylvia.

WAITRESS. Hi Chip. Pay up.

CHIP. Keep the change!

WAITRESS. See you later, Sly.

> *(sings)*
>
> I GO OUT DRIVING, AFTER MIDNIGHT, SEARCHIN
> FOR YOU...
>
> *(She blows **SLY** a kiss. **CHIP** catches it and gobbles it up. He winks at the **WAITRESS**.)*

WAITRESS. I just threw up in my mouth a little bit.

> *(The **WAITRESS** exits. **SLY** shakes his head.)*

CHIP. She's gonna be ex-wife #5.

> (**SLY** *shakes his head.*)

CHIP. So, you ever been married?

> (**SLY** *shakes his head.*)
>
> So you got like a girlfriend or anything?
>
> (**SLY** *shakes his head.*)
>
> How bout ladies? You got "ladies?"
>
> (**SLY** *smiles.*)
>
> Of course you do.
>
> (**SLY** *shrugs.*)
>
> You ever cheat?

SLY. If you don't cheat, you look like an idiot.

CHIP. Huh?

SLY. If you do it and you don't get caught, you look like a hero. If you do it and you get caught, you look like a dope. Put me in the category where I belong.

CHIP. You know, man, I like you.

> You got something to you.
>
> You're, aww nevermind.
>
> I don't know what it is about you.
>
> You know, I just like you. I like being around you. You know what I'm saying man?

SLY. What?

> (**CHIP** *puts his arm around* **SLY**, *gives him a big bear-hug.*)

CHIP. Man, I just, like you.

SLY. Like me?

CHIP. You know, yeah, like not "like that" or anything.

SLY. Yeah man, sure.

> (*pause*)

CHIP. Can I buy you another?

> (*Engine sounds roar as we transition to the track.*)

SCENE NINE: May the Best Man Win

(**HOTSHOT** *and* **LEGS**. *Just before the race. Isolated in two spotlights.*)

HOTSHOT. You look a little nervous.

LEGS. Just thinking.

HOTSHOT. The gas is on the right, the brake is on the left.

LEGS. Thinking about what I'm gonna buy with my prize money.

HOTSHOT. Don't spend it yet. Can I see your helmet?

LEGS. Sure.

(*She throws it to him. He catches.*)

HOTSHOT. Light as a feather.

LEGS. What did ya think? It was made outta lead?
What's that in your pocket? Is that some kinda wedge or you just happy to see me?

HOTSHOT. No sore losers right?
What do you say we up the ante?

LEGS. Double or nothing?

HOTSHOT. If I win, you take me out on the town.

LEGS. If I win, I get one of those kisses you keep bragging about.

HOTSHOT. A kiss huh? I could give you that right now.

LEGS. In the winner's circle. On Victory Lane.

HOTSHOT. You drive a hard bargain.

LEGS. May the best man win.

(**LEGS** *puts her helmet on and exits.*)

HOTSHOT. Women.

(*Transition to* **RICHARD** *and* **RANDY** *mid-broadcast.*)

SCENE TEN: Tit for Tat

(LOUD ENGINE SOUNDS. REALLY LOUD. DEAF-ENING. **RICHARD** *enters, zipping his fly.)*

RANDY. Welcome back, NASCAR fans, and welcome back, Richey boy.

RICHARD. Thank you Randy – Oh! Looks like HOTSHOT #7, Big Red Gum Ford is still leading the pack here at the Fontana Fresh Squeeze Superspeedway.

RANDY. Have a seat.

*(***RICHARD*** *sits on a whoopee cushion* **RANDY** *has placed on his chair!)*

RANDY. WOOOOOWWWWWWWWWWWWEEEEEEEEEEE! Look at them go.

*(***RICHARD*** *sits in silent embarrassment.)*

RANDY. Hooo Hoo! With his daddy, Rocky Kane the pole sitter closing in fast on his BUTTOX. Eh, Richey? And L'eggs Pantyhose in hot pursuit.

RICHARD. Followed by 47, 24, 13, 29, 62

RANDY. SOLD!

RICHARD. 4 laps from the finish.

RANDY. And, speaking of legs, she's got 'um.

RICHARD. She holds a Ph.D. in physics –

RANDY. She's holds a Ph.D. in knockers I'll tell you that. She's got an advanced degree.

RICHARD. Well driven! Well driven! As she challenges Hotshot Big Red Gum Ford for the lead.

RANDY. There weren't girls on the track in my day. They couldn't cut it then, and they can't cut it now.

RICHARD. And that from a man who never won a championship in his entire racing career.

*(***RANDY*** *is silent. Fierce silence.)*

RICHARD. And Legs Nelson setting a blistering pace with Hotshot Kenny Kane the 3rd. They are neck and neck.

(He glances at **RANDY** *who is still stewing.)*

Boogidy boogidy boogidy!

SCENE ELEVEN: The Inspector Inspects

(In the garage. Legs Nelson's car is being inspected. She paints her nails.)

MAN IN THE HAT. This is an American sport, Ms. Nelson. Where every automobile is created equal. Where every racer has an equal opportunity to win.

LEGS. Like I won again? Fair and square?

(THE INSPECTOR requests his tools like a doctor preparing for a surgical strike. THE MAN IN THE HAT hands the items to THE INSPECTOR.)

INSPECTOR. Glofs.

MAN IN THE HAT. It's typical, Ms. Nelson.

LEGS. Typical?

MAN IN THE HAT. To dig a little deeper.

INSPECTOR. Rhul-air.

MAN IN THE HAT. If there's a certain Chevrolet. Or Ford.

LEGS. Or female?

MAN IN THE HAT. Or racer, who's getting ahead.

INSPECTOR. Magnifying gless.

MAN IN THE HAT. You know, on a winning streak –

LEGS. You mean beating the pants off the men.

INSPECTOR. Dental floss.

MAN IN THE HAT. I mean, we have to make sure that no one -

INSPECTOR. Is shitting!

MAN IN THE HAT. Has any unfair advantage.

INSPECTOR. Dental floss!

MAN IN THE HAT. We need to reassure our television viewers that this is a fair sport –

INSPECTOR. Chewing gum.

MAN IN THE HAT. An American sport –

LEGS. Well I can assure you, gentlemen –

MAN IN THE HAT. Believe me, I want to believe you.

INSPECTOR. Ah-hah!

MAN IN THE HAT. What?

INSPECTOR. It is not zee uhrl.

LEGS. Of course it's not the oil.

INSPECTOR. AH HAH!

MAN IN THE HAT. What?

INSPECTOR. It is not zee tiers.

MAN IN THE HAT. Your tires are fine.

LEGS. This is ridiculous.

INSPECTOR. Ah hah!

MAN IN THE HAT. What?

INSPECTOR. We must take apart zee engyna.

MAN IN THE HAT. Well now, I don't think we need to go through all that.

INSPECTOR. Zis sing zat goes like zis.

MAN IN THE HAT. Tweezers?

INSPECTOR. Yes.

Ze sing zat gos like zat.

MAN IN THE HAT. Hair dryer?

LEGS. This is totally unacceptable.

Taking every piece of an engine, and laying it out for God and everybody to see?

MAN IN THE HAT. I agree. Do you have to strip her down to the bare block in public?

(The **INSPECTOR** *raises a finger.)*

INSPECTOR. AH-hah!

MAN IN THE HAT & LEGS. What?

INSPECTOR. Eversing iz according to zee rhule book. She is okay *(holds up the hand sign for okay).* Okie dokie. A # 1.

MAN IN THE HAT. Well, Congratulations Miss Nelson.

LEGS. Thank you.

MAN IN THE HAT. My sincerest apologies to you and L'eggs Pantyhose, Honey Bunn. See you in Victory Lane!

INSPECTOR. But.

MAN IN THE HAT. But?

INSPECTOR. Schtill, zer is somesing stranch.

MAN IN THE HAT. Stranch?

INSPECTOR. I intuit somesing stranch.

LEGS. But you said everything was a-okay.

INSPECTOR. Okie-dokie. Yes, I zaid zo.

LEGS. You zaid zo.

INSPECTOR. But I donut nozo.

MAN INTHE HAT. Donut nozo?

INSPECTOR. Yes, Everysing iz zee right size. But.

MAN IN THE HAT. But?

LEGS. But?

INSPECTOR. But.

LEGS. But what?

MAN IN THE HAT. What?

INSPECTOR. What?

LEGS. What but?

MAN IN THE HAT. Her butt?

INSPECTOR. Butt?

LEGS. But what is it?

MAN IN THE HAT. What!!?

INSPECTOR. Exactly.

SCENE TWELVE: Fans and Winners

(**RICHARD** *and* **RANDY** *announce.*)

RANDY. They're front to bumper – bumper to front –

(*A* **NAKED FAN** *streaks across the scene.*)

Whoa!

RICHARD. Whoa what was that?

RANDY. That's a naked fan!

RICHARD. Streaking through the stands!

RANDY. That is a genuine all-American dedicated NASCAR fan.

RICHARD. I tell you, it's the FANS.

RANDY. It is, it is. It's the FANS that make this sport a sight to see!

RICHARD. They come in all shapes and sizes.

RANDY. They come in short shorts and halter tops. God bless 'um.

RICHARD. They come from every state across America!

RANDY. They come in teeny weeny bikinis with teeny tiny hinies!

RICHARD. It's the fans that make the drivers!

RANDY. You know once when I was just starting out a 15 year old girl in a bikini put her teeny little hinie –

RICHARD. AND THEY'RE HEATING UP THE POCONOS WITH JUST TEN LAPS TO GO –

(**THE FANS** *enter one by one. They are decked out in race regalia, souvenirs and flags.* **FLIP**, *the father, carries an enormous cooler. He's followed by* **CASSIE**. *They make their way through the audience, and take their seat on a bench – the race-way bleachers. They engage the audience.*)

CASSIE. I feel the need! –

FLIP. (*to man in audience*) Smell that Rubber BURN! –

CASSIE. The need for speed! –

FLIP. You can't get this at home in front of the TV, Pal. –

CASSIE. Woooooooooo! –

FLIP. I'm Flip, Niceta Meetcha. Where's Joany?

CASSIE. WOOOOOOOO!

FLIP. That's my kid – Cassie.

CASSIE. *(to boy in audience.)* HEY JORDAN! YOUR BOY IS LOSING! –

FLIP. Want a beer? –

CASSIE. HE'S SUCKING TAILPIPE! WOOOOO! –

FLIP. Joany!

CASSIE. WILD-ASSED WILD-ASSED! WOOOOOOO!

FLIP. Cassie.

> (**JOANY** *enters, a pair of L'eggs Pantyhose on her head – to show her support.*)

JOANY. Cassie Honey put some clothes on, you're getting a sunburn.

> *(She turns to the audience.)*

Hi, I'm Joany. We're from Chicago. You? –

FLIP. I see you like #47.

JOANY. YOU GO LEGS!

FLIP. He's my guy too #47!

JOANY. L'EGGS PANTYHOSE! THAT A' GIRL!

FLIP. FIGHT FOR IT ROCKY! FIGHT FOR IT! –

He's a veteran –

JOANY. 50 bucks says L'eggs Pantyhose wins the checkered. –

FLIP. He started this sport. –

JOANY. What do you say? 50 bucks. –

FLIP. HERE THEY COME.

> (**MITCHY** *enters with* **GRANDMA**. **GRANDMA** *moves incredibly slowly. It takes her 4 pages to make her way to a seat. She's nearly blown over by passing cars and crashes.*)

CASSIE. FASTER!

JOANY. SOCK IT TO, UM LEGS PANTYHOSE! GET'ER DONE! WOOOO!

FLIP. *(getting drowned out by the sound of the race cars passing)* YEAH I BROUGHT THE WHOLE FAMILY IN MY BIG

(Vvrrrrrrrrrrrooooooooom)

NASCAR TOUR. WHO THE HECK WOULDA THOUGHT

(Vrrrrrrrooooooooom)

BONDING EXPERIENCE, BUT GRANDMA –

(Vrrrrrrooooooooooooooom)

THE WHOLE SUMMER LONG. ANYWHERE THEY

(Vvvvvvvvrrrrrrooooom)

WE FOLLOW. BRATWORST?

(The sound of a huge CRASH.)

JOANY. Oh!

CASSIE. They're crashing, Daddy!

(CRASH)

CASSIE. I love it when they crash!

(CRASH)

CASSIE. Yes!

MITCHIE. Die.

(CRASH)

CASSIE. YES! YES!

MITCHIE. Die. Die.

(CRASH. CRASH.)

CASSIE. *(singing)* HIT ME BABY ONE MORE TIME!

FLIP. Turn on your radios, Joany! Mitchie!

*(Actor playing **JOANY** holds a transistor radio up as if she's listening. From behind the radio, she speaks as **RANDY**.)*

FLIP. *(to the radio)* WHAT HAPPENED! TELL US WHAT HAPPENED!

> *(Actor playing* **MITCHY** *holds the radio up to cover as she speaks as* **RICHARD**.)*

RANDY. *(on the radio)* Wholey moley will you look at that.

RICHARD.	**RANDY.**
What a crash.	Holey moley!
Wow	whoa
Look at that.	Will you look at that.

FLIP. Come on!

> You call that commentary?
>
> Tell us what's happening Asshole!

RICHARD.	**RANDY.**
Lot's of smoke.	Bum deal!
Too bad	Bummer, bummer.
And the Caution Flag	Caution Flag, Caution
is out.	Flag.

FLIP. We can see that!

> We know that Einstein!
>
> And they get paid for this?

CASSIE. Tell us something we don't know, Asshole!

JOANY. Cassie, language.

CASSIE. What? Dad says it –

FLIP. Shhhhhhhh.

RICHARD. Let's cut away to the cutaway cam car camera –

> *(***JOANY*** switches to* **CHIP***.)*

CHIP. Yeah, I really thought we had this one, Randy, guess we just run outta luck when our Lucky Charms Engine blew up. –

> *(Back to* **JOANY***)*

CASSIE. YOUR BOY BLEW AN ENGINE, JORDAN!

FLIP. Under caution with 3 laps to go. Exciting stuff, huh?

CASSIE. This is soooooo slow.

JOANY. Flip, pass me up a Bud Light.

CASSIE. Why can't they speed up?

JOANY. Cassie Honey, people are hurt.

CASSIE. SPEED UP!

JOANY. Where's my eyeliner?

CASSIE. Ask Michelle.

MITCHIE. Mitchell.

JOANY. Mitchie, if you borrow my eyeliner you need to put it back in my purse when you're finished.

FLIP. Put on your race shirt, Mitch, you're being unsociable.

My son, he's a little on the strange side.

Have a brat, boy.

MITCHIE. I don't eat flesh.

JOANY. It's a hotdog Mitchie, you eat hotdogs. Where is my lighter, I swear it was in here. And lose the stupid Billy Idol accent.

MITCHIE. Is Grandma dead?

JOANY. Shhh. She's napping, Mitchie. Don't wake her.

    (VROOOOOOOOOOOOOM! The cars race by. **CASSIE** *is busy showing a man in the audience/grandstand the drivers' autographs on her body.)*

CASSIE. *(to man in audience)* Yeah, I got Marvin Martin, Martin Sterling, Sterling Marlin and Chip Chowalsky, Charlie Chipman, Oh, that's a tattoo and I'm gonna get the whole pit crew to sign right here –

JOANY. Cassie! Oh, hi. Sorry, she's –

CASSIE. We're staying on the infield. My dad got us a Winnebago just for this –

JOANY. CASSIE! GREEN FLAG!

CASSIE. THEY'RE GOING! THEY'RE GOING! WOOOOOOO YEAH! GO FAST GO FAST!

FLIP. Here comes your girl, Joany!

JOANY. YOU GO GIRLFRIEND!

CASSIE. Mom! You are sooooooo embarrassing me.

JOANY. YOU GO GIRL!

CASSIE. I hate her.

JOANY. SHE IS IT! SUPPORT HOSE RULES, BABY!

CASSIE. Cheater.

JOANY. HERE SHE COMES HERE COMES THE CHECK-ERS, LEGS! YOU GO GIRL!

I think I just peed a little!

(*JOANY exits towards Victory Lane, ecstatic.*)

FLIP. You won it Joany!

Joany?

Where'd your mother go, Cassie?

CASSIE. She is not my mother.

FLIP. This is going to be an awesome summer, kids!

Hey Bob! Looks like you got a new grill there! A Propane 600 Firestarter Plus, huh? Mind if I come over for a brewski?

(*He exits. CASSIE and MITCHELL sit in silence. He stares at her.*)

CASSIE. Shut-up.

(*He is silent.*)

Stop looking at me. Creep.

MITCHIE. (*reciting his poetry, playing with his lighter*) Death stalks the track. Like a hunter. When every car explodes in red lizard tongue flames and the track is slick with oil, a spark ignites pit road. And souls scream.

CASSIE. You're such a creep. Go blow up a high-school homo bomber.

(*MITCHIE exits.*)

(*CASSIE sees CHIP.*)

CHIP! CHIP! CHOWALSKY! SIGN MY BODY! I WANT TO HAVE YOUR BABY! I MEAN AFTER THIS ONE!

(*She looks up at a teletron.*)

Oh my god, is that our Mom on Victory Lane? (*sniff*) C'mon Grandma, we gotta change your pampers.

(Transition to Victory Lane. Live or on video.)

LEGS. We had a good race, Dick, I had a fast car, thanks to my –

(JOANY *butts in.)*

JOANY. L'EEEEEEEGGGGGGGS PANTYHOSE!! I WILL NEVER WEAR ANYTHING ELSE! WOOOOOOOOO!

LEGS. It was a team effort, Richard –

JOANY. Legs, Legs, girlfriend, you are my hero, you are breaking barriers sweetheart, speed barriers, gender barriers, and you are one hot babe too!

LEGS. I'm really proud of everyone – we did it, time to celebrate –

JOANY. *(shoving a pantyhose egg at* **LEGS***)* Can you sign this for my daughter, Hon, you are so inspiring to her. Just kiss it!

(to the camera)

CASSIE, LOOK AT THIS! You can be anything you want to be with L'eggs Sheer Energy! HOLLY LEGS NELSON! SHE IS MY GIIIIIRRRRRLLLLL-FRIEND! L'EGGS PANTYHOSE SHEAR ENERGY! WOOOOOOOOO! Ooh, I think I just peed again.

(Crossfade to a shady location.)

SCENE THIRTEEN: Over

(Lights up on **ROCKY** *and* **CHICKEN** 1. *After the race.)*

CHICKEN 1. It's over!

ROCKY. What are you talking about, over?

CHICKEN 1. It's over.

ROCKY. Why?

CHICKEN 1. Over.

ROCKY. But I could win this season, I got a chance –

CHICKEN 1. Over.

ROCKY. It ain't over.

CHICKEN 1. Over.

ROCKY. It ain't over.

(The **CHICKEN** *rips contract.)*

ROCKY. Fucking Chicken.

CHIP. Sorry man.

SCENE FOURTEEN: Mustache

(The #8 car is parked in the garage, the hood is up. An unidentifiable Shadowy Figure slinks about the garage. A knock on the door. The Shadowy Figure exits. No answer. Another knock.)

SLY. Holly?

*(**SLY** pokes his head in the door.)*

SLY. Legs?

*(No answer. **SLY** slips in the door. Looks around. No Holly. No one's around. Sly inspects the car. Working fast, inspects a strange-looking spring on the back of the car, looks under the hood. [sound effect BOING.] **LEGS** enters. Watches **SLY** who is absorbed in her engine.)*

LEGS. See anything you like?

SLY. *(startled)* Oh!

LEGS. Anything unusual?

SLY. I was just looking –

LEGS. I can see that.

SLY. For you.

LEGS. I'm not under the hood.

SLY. Alright, you caught me- -

LEGS. Red-handed.

SLY. Sorry. I really stopped by to see -

LEGS. The inside of my engine?

SLY. Look, I know you're in the hotseat.
I just stopped by to tell you –

LEGS. To tell me –

SLY. I'm starting to respect you.

LEGS. Starting?

SLY. To admire you.

LEGS. Should I be impressed?

SLY. It's about time a woman really took the cake.

LEGS. So you're impressed cuz I'm a woman.

SLY. I don't think you're cheating.

LEGS. Oh really?

SLY. I think you're the real thing.

LEGS. As opposed to what?

SLY. You're like Amelia Earhart and Sally Ride or…Oprah Winfrey. You're going where no woman's gone before. I want to see you do it, I want you to take the cup, to win the whole series, I should be racing you, but I'm in your corner. When we made that move together on the track, zoom-zoom, it was a rush, when I think about you crossing that line first, my heart races, I can't catch my breath, my pulse is through the roof, when you win, I want to celebrate, it's adrenalin, it's joy, when you win, I'm on top of the world!

(pause)

*(**LEGS** looks at **SLY**.)*

(pause)

SLY. What?

LEGS. Just looking.

SLY. At what?

LEGS. You.

SLY. What about me?

LEGS. I don't think I've ever heard you say so many words all in a row.

*(**LEGS** pursues **SLY**.)*

SLY. Oh.

(back peddling)

Guess I got excited?

LEGS. I know what you mean.

SLY. Guess I trust you?

LEGS. I liked it when you taught me your Karaoke moves.

SLY. Rumors are starting.

LEGS. Are they true?

SLY. Uh. No.

LEGS. Are we racing here?

SLY. Racing?

LEGS. *(testing* **SLY***)* Are you racing me?

SLY. No, what? – I just –

> *(She kisses* **SLY***. "His" mustache comes off. Falls to the floor.*
>
> **LEGS** *screams.)*

LEGS. OH MY GOD!

SLY. What?

> *(***SLY*** sees her mustache on the floor.)*

OH! A spider!

> *(***SLY*** steps on the mustache. Covers her face – where the mustache would have been.)*

LEGS. What's wrong with your mouth? Sly?

SLY. What?

LEGS. Oh my god. You're a –

SLY. What? I'm a what?

LEGS. You're a?

SLY. I'm just trying to make it, Holly, I'm just trying to race.

LEGS. What are you?

SLY. A woman. I'm a woman.

LEGS. AGHHHHH!

SLY. Well so are you!

LEGS. But I've always been a woman!

SLY. Shhhhh. Can you help me, Holly? Help me out here.

LEGS. I thought I was the only woman on this circuit.

SLY. Listen, women don't make it.

LEGS. I make it.

SLY. You got money, you got L'eggs Pantyhose. I need sponsors, you don't understand.

I'm just doing what it takes.

LEGS. But -

SLY. Shhh…Don't blow my cover.

LEGS. Who are you?

SLY. I'm Wendy and I meant what I said. That I want you to win it. You help me, I help you, okay? I help you win it.

LEGS. I'm just a little. In shock, Wendy. I thought I was the only –

SLY. Do it for us.

LEGS. For us?

(**WENDY** *puts her shades back on, disguising herself as* **SLY** *again.*)

SLY. Deal?

(*Lights fade. Car engine sounds. Transition to* **RICHARD** *and* **RANDY** *on the air.*)

SCENE FIFTEEN: Crash

(RANDY vamps to cover costume change for RICHARD.)

RANDY. Well, butter my butt and call me a biscuit.

It's been hotter'n a goat's butt in a pepper patch.

So dry, the trees are bribing the dogs.

This is gooder'n grits.

If it gets any better I may have to hire someone to help me enjoy it.

(RICHARD interrupts.)

RICHARD. I'm ready.

RANDY. Then here we go. They are neck and neck, shoulder to shoulder, head to head –

RICHARD. Father and Son.

RANDY. Battling it out in the Bristol heat!

RICHARD. Like Oedipus and his Daddy.

RANDY. Like me and my Daddy back in '72.

RICHARD. Racing is epic folks, it's Freudian.

RANDY. It's what?

RICHARD. It's Historical! It's Greek, it's cutthroat blood vengeance.

RANDY. Hell, it's RACING! I know what he's going through, I remember the first time I beat my Daddy in a race, I got a wupping –

RICHARD. Must be hard to have it all in the family.

RANDY. What?

RICHARD. My father's an astrophysicist

RANDY. Ouch! He should get that biop-sied.

RICHARD. 3 laps left to go.

RANDY. It doesn't get any better than this!

(The deafening sound of engines. Hectic. End of a race. On the track. The racers in their rolling "stock car" chairs.)

ROCKY. Come on

HOTSHOT. What's it gonna be

ROCKY. Win or die tryin

HOTSHOT. Win

ROCKY. Or go out fightin

CHIP. Come on

SLY. Turn two!

> *(They each lean into the turn as they round the corner. It's* **HOTSHOT** *first, followed by* **LEGS**, **SLY**, **ROCKY** *and…* **CHIP**.*)*

HOTSHOT. I'm too loose.

LEGS. I'm ready to move –

SLY. On turn four, wait for me.

> *(***ROCKY*** creeps up on* **HOTSHOT**.*)*

ROCKY. I'm right on your tail, Son.

I'm coming up behind you.

CHIP. Come on, come on.

SLY. Now!

LEGS. I got him.

SLY. We got him.

> *(***LEGS*** and* **SLY** *slingshot past* **HOTSHOT**.*)*

HOTSHOT. Damn.

LEGS & SLY. Woooooowwwweeeeee

HOTSHOT. Not so fast, Honeybunny.

CHIP. What's with my engine!

SLY. I'm outta gas. I'm comin' in.

> *(***SLY*** spins upstage out of the race.)*

LEGS. See ya later.

CHIP. She's smoking like Havana cigar.

Jimminy Christmas, to win a race, you got to finish a race, Fellas.

> *(***CHIP*** spins out of the race.)*

> *(Now it's* **LEGS** *leading, followed by* **HOTSHOT**, *followed by* **ROCKY**.*)*

ROCKY. Come on Son.

LEGS. Take it easy back there.

ROCKY. Show me what you got, kid.

HOTSHOT. Don't get reckless now –

ROCKY. Show me you're not all mouth.

HOTSHOT. Keep your temper.

Take it easy –

(**ROCKY** *bumps* **HOTSHOT** *from behind, trying to pass.* **HOTSHOT** *loses control. Then* **ROCKY** *loses control.*)

HOTSHOT. Whoa!

ROCKY. Whoa!

HOTSHOT. What the hell?

LEGS. Go low!

Go low!

(*The racers spin in their stock car chairs.*)

(*Blackout. HUGE CRASH. Lights up on* **RANDY** *announcing the aftermath of the crash.* **RICHARD** *is noticeably silent. Horrified.*)

RANDY. He's not getting outta the car, listen to this crowd going crazy, Eh Richey? Woooohooo, this is racing! SMACK! SLAM! SHAZAM! Goodness gracious GREAT BALLS OF FIRE! The 'Ol Man was trying to take his son out, but he sent them both up into the wall. This is racing, Eh Dickey? Somebody might be mincemeat down there in that mess. WHACK! WHAM! WOWEEE! This is what this sport is all about. NASCAR, because for all the other sports you only need one ball! Let's watch that again! Dickey, hand me another hotdog, will ya?

(*Music plays as lights rise on the garage.*)

SCENE SIXTEEN: Inspector Returns

(In the garage. **THE INSPECTOR** *and* **THE MAN IN THE HAT** *inspect* **LEGS NELSON**'s *engine. Again.)*

INSPECTOR. It is very stranch.

MAN IN THE HAT. Stranch?

INSPECTOR. Still… zer is somesing stranch.

MAN IN THE HAT. Stranch?

INSPECTOR. Yes, Everysing iz zee right size.

LEGS. Good, can I go?

INSPECTOR. But.

MAN IN THE HAT. But?

INSPECTOR. Ah-ha! Bring zee scal!

MAN IN THE HAT. Speak American, Goddamn it.

INSPECTOR. Zee scal!

LEGS. You saw what happened out there! I got people I got to talk to –

INSPECTOR. Ah-ha! Now we weh zee piss.

MAN IN THE HAT. What piss?

INSPECTOR. Zis piss. I am very specicious of zis piss.

LEGS. You have drivers out there who hit the wall, went up on fire –

MAN IN THE HAT. That's the sport, Honey-bun, that's why folks watch it.

LEGS. Do you care what's happening out there to your drivers?

MAN IN THE HAT. Sit down Ms. Nelson. And be a lady.

(The **INSPECTOR** *places the small metal engine piece on the scale.)*

INSPECTOR. AH-HA! WHALLAH! ZEE PISS'S WET.

MAN IN THE HAT. *(trying to joke with the* **INSPECTOR***)* Of course it's wet, it's piss.

INSPECTOR. The Piss, she is too lat!

LEGS. This is ridiculous –

INSPECTOR. Yes! To zee ass it is a normal piss. But zee scal can tell it is a too lit piss. It is fooling zee ass.

MAN IN THE HAT. Zee ass? Goddamn it.

INSPECTOR. The ASS!

(*The* INSPECTOR *points to his eyes.*)

MAN IN THE HAT. Oh! Fooling zee eyes?! Jesus Christmas.

INSPECTOR. Ah-ha! Take another piss!

MAN IN THE HAT. You mean it's not just that piss, Ms. Nelson?

LEGS. Can we do this later?

MAN IN THE HAT. What are you playing with here, Lady?

INSPECTOR. Spes.

MAN IN THE HAT. Spes?

INSPECTOR. Ooterspes.

MAN IN THE HAT. Are you saying this is alien stuff?

INSPECTOR. Spes age material. Med for ooter spes. For making a spes ship, not a zrooooom. Automobile. Zis metal is for men in spes.

MAN IN THE HAT. I've had about enough of this alien shenanigans.

LEGS. It's a new lightweight alloy, gentlemen, it spins faster on the inside, making more power so the car goes faster.

MAN IN THE HAT. We know that, Lady, we've seen this before!

(*whispers to* INSPECTOR)

Have we seen this before?

LEGS. I invented it.

INSPECTOR. Oh really? Smat cookie.

LEGS. Now can I go?

MAN IN THE HAT. I'm afraid that's shitting!

INSPECTOR. Shitting?

MAN IN THE HAT. Goddamn it, now I'm doing it too. That's cheating, Ms. Nelson. Illegal.

LEGS. There's not a rule against it.

MAN IN THE HAT. Well, there is now.

(He writes down.)

Absolutely no. What do you call that stuff?

LEGS. Nelsonium.

MAN IN THE HAT. Absolutely no nelsonium.

LEGS. Great. I'll remember that.

(She goes to exit.)

INSPECTOR. Ah-ha!

MAN IN THE HAT. Hold on Honey-bun!

LEGS. What now?

INSPECTOR. I'm afrid you are disqualified Mz. Nelson.

LEGS. It's not against the rules, cuz no one's ever heard of it, we covered that –

INSPECTOR. That piss is not against the ruhlbook. But ZIS IS.

(The INSPECTOR holds up a test-tube full of fuel.)

MAN IN THE HAT. Zis piss?

LEGS. What is that?

INSPECTOR. Is no piss.

(Transition to CHIP's garage.)

SCENE SEVENTEEN: Chicken 2

(**CHIP** *works under his car. A chicken emerges from the shadows. This is a different chicken. Same suit. This chicken is a tough chicken. This is* **CHICKEN 2**.)

CHICKEN 2. BAWK!

(**CHIP** *startles.*)

CHICKEN 2. You didn't win.

CHIP. Yeah, you know my engine –

CHICKEN 2. You were supposed to win.

CHIP. What do you mean supposed to win?

CHICKEN 2. I mean, everybody else gets taken out and you can't even finish?

You're giving Chicken a bad name, Pal.

CHIP. Wait a minute –

CHICKEN 2. I don't have a minute.

CHIP. You're not the same chicken.

CHICKEN 2. Same chicken as who?

CHIP. Same chicken I talked to last time –

CHICKEN 2. You want to talk chicken, let's talk chicken –

CHIP. I don't want to talk chicken.

CHICKEN 2. Tell that to a little child sitting in front of the TV with a mouth full of chicken, crying his head off because his chicken is losing. See, in his mind, he's associating CHICKEN with LOSER. Loser/Chicken, Loser/Chicken, Chicken/Loser. And he's gonna grow up hating chicken. You're breeding a whole generation of chicken haters. You son of a bitch.

CHIP. Whoa, take it easy.

CHICKEN 2. Come'ere.

CHIP. No.

CHICKEN 2. Come'ere.

CHIP. Why?

CHICKEN 2. I'm not gonna hurtcha. Come're –

CHIP. Why should I?

CHICKEN 2. Chicken.

CHIP. Who you calling Chicken?

CHICKEN 2. BAWK BAWK BAWK BAWK

CHIP. You think that's funny?

CHICKEN 2. CLUCK CLUCK CLUCK CLUCK

CHIP. Come'ere.

CHICKEN 2. *(mocking him)* Come'ere

CHIP. Come on!

CHICKEN 2. *(mocking him)* Come on!

CHIP. Right now, chicken!

CHICKEN 2. I don't like the way you said that word.

CHIP. BAWK BAWK BAWK BAWK, CLUCK CLUCK CLUCK.

> *(The **CHICKEN** lunges at **CHIP**. An all-out brawl. Feathers fly.)*

CHICKEN 2. This is for the children!

> *(**CHICKEN 2** slams **CHIP**'s head on something hard.)*

Promise you'll win.

CHIP. Alright! I promise! I promise!

CHICKEN 2. Promise what?

> *(Slams **CHIP**'s head again.)*

CHIP. That I'll try.

> *(Slams **CHIP**'s head twice.)*

CHIP. That I'll win.

> *(**CHICKEN 2** punches **CHIP** in the gut. **CHIP** crumbles.)*

CHICKEN 2. You better win, Chowalsky. *(Kicks **CHIP**.)*

Or your gonna see me every where you turn, I'll be in your breakfast cereal in the morning, in your shower, and in your bed at night. I'm gonna stick to you like stink on doo doo. *(Stomps on **CHIP**.)* I'm gonna be your nightmare.

> *(**CHICKEN 2** exits, leaving **CHIP** on the floor in a pile of feathers.)*

CHIP. Fucking chicken.

> *(Transition to the Karaoke Bar.)*

SCENE EIGHTEEN: Cheatin' Car

(**HOTSHOT** and **THE WAITRESS**. *In a bar. Again, different Karaoke bar, but it looks exactly the same...except for a sign that says, "THE THIRSTY FRUITFLY."* **HOTSHOT** *throws darts alone.* **THE WAITRESS** *watches him.*)

HOTSHOT. You see the sky, you see the ground, you see the sky, you see the ground.

You know when it gets quiet, you're in trouble

Cuz you're in the air, and you've got to come down.

You feel every hit. You take a lot of hits. You tense all your muscles up.

WAITRESS. Did you see that white light?

HOTSHOT. Nope. It was lonely, Sylvia.

WAITRESS. Did you see God? What'd he look like?

HOTSHOT. Didn't see him.

WAITRESS. I think a near death experience is sexy.

How's your daddy?

HOTSHOT. Hospital's keeping him overnight.

WAITRESS. Don't worry about that ol' Veteran, he's survived worse.

What do you say we dance, put on some Elvis?

HOTSHOT. You know, there's a woman like you in every town. She's always a waitress and she's always named Sylvia.

WAITRESS. No, it's just me. I'm following you.

(**LEGS** *enters.*)

LEGS. If you can't beat 'um, take 'um out of the game, right?

HOSTHOT. Holly, I've been thinking – life's too short, you're talented, good looking, and a damn good driver, I respect you, I admire you and I like you, so let's just cut this competition crap and get this first kiss out of the way.

LEGS. Unbelievable.

HOTSHOT. What'd I do?

LEGS. They found Cocamydopropyl in my catch can.

HOTSHOT. They found what now?

LEGS. Shampoo.

WAITRESS. Uh-oh.

LEGS. Took me and my Pantyhose Chevy out of the season. You're a sore loser, you know that?

HOTSHOT. You think I sabotaged your car?

LEGS. You did sabotage my car.

HOTSHOT. Nice of you to ask how I'm doing.

LEGS. Well, someone did.

HOTSHOT. And it looks like my Daddy's gonna make it too. I'll tell him you asked about him.

LEGS. I was getting around to that.

WAITRESS. Shampoo. Well I heard –

LEGS. Nobody asked you.

WAITRESS. It's none of my business. Y'all work it out.

(*The* **WAITRESS** *exits.*)

LEGS. If I'd have known what you're capable of –

HOTSHOT. It's part of the game, Honey, watching your back.

LEGS. Couldn't take it, huh?

HOTSHOT. Couldn't cut it, huh?

LEGS. Couldn't play fair?

HOTSHOT. Couldn't last a season?

LEGS. Couldn't beat me straight?

HOTSHOT. Well, maybe you deserved it.

LEGS. Deserved it?

HOTSHOT. Well, you're not very well liked.

(**LEGS** *picks up the Karaoke microphone. Sings.*)

YOUR CHEATIN' CAR (based on Your Cheatin' Heart by Hank Williams)

LEGS.

YOUR CHEATIN' CAR WILL MAKE YOU WEEP
YOU KNOW INSIDE, THAT YOU'RE A CREEP
YOU'VE GOT TO CHEAT, CUZ I'M BETTER'N YOU
YOUR CHEATIN' CAR WILL TELL ON YOU

(**HOTSHOT** *takes the microphone.*)

HOTSHOT.
WHEN YOUR CAR EXPLODES LIKE A HAND GRENADE
YOU'LL FALL APART AND CALL MY NAME
YOU BETTER FILL YOUR TANK
WITH MORE SHAMPOO
YOUR CHEATIN' CAR WILL TELL ON YOU

LEGS. You're gonna be sorry you sang that.

(**LEGS** *exits.* **WAITRESS** *grabs the microphone, sings:*)

WAITRESS.
WHEN HER CAR EXPLODES LIKE A HAND GRENADE

HOTSHOT.
SHE'LL FALL APART AND CALL MY NAME

WAITRESS.
SHE'S GONNA WISH SHE DID DONE DROVE LIKE YOU

HOTSHOT & WAITRESS.
HER CHEATIN' CAR WON'T PULL HER THROUGH.

(*The* **WAITRESS** *hands him a beer and leans into him as the music plays on.*)

WAITRESS. Here. It's on the house.

I almost died once too. In a blue Buick on Hwy 32. Saw those white lights. Headlights. Are you listening to me, Sugar?

HOTSHOT. I'm not gonna chase her.

WAITRESS. Woowee, sabotage huh?

HOTSHOT. It wasn't me.

WAITRESS. I know you didn't do it, Honey.

(*He looks at her.*)

I'm not saying I know who did.

HOTSHOT. Who?

SCENE NINETEEN: Can o' Worms

(The sound of stock car engines.)

RANDY. Well, the girl cheated, the old man exploded and the Hotshot is looking lukewarm, who the hell does that leave us with down there, Dickey Doodle?

RICHARD. Well.

RANDY. Well?

*(**RICHARD** is silent.)*

You're awful quiet there, Dick, got something stuck in your pie hole?

RICHARD. Well, Randy, after the recent disappointments, the accusations of cheating, the recent spike in the price of oil, and the seemingly never-ending war, I've been ruminating on racing –

RANDY. Ruminating, well, hell Dick, spit it out, enlighten us –

RICHARD. Well, I'd hate to create a controversy but –

RANDY. I smell me a can of worms.

RICHARD. But, are drivers really athletes?

RANDY. Uh-oh. Them's fightin' words, Bubba.

RICHARD. Can't any idiot step on a gas pedal?

RANDY. Why don't you tell the folks at home how you really feel.

RICHARD. I feel that we're perpetuating America's obsession with violence and I feel that we're USING these athletes –

RANDY. So now they're athletes, huh?

RICHARD. USING them as billboards to sell beer, Cheerios, Viagra –

RANDY. They weren't "athletes" a minute ago folks – "any idiot can step on a gas pedal."

RICHARD. And where are the African-American drivers? Why aren't there more women and people of color? Where are the Filipino drivers and Chinese American drivers and the Filipino Chinese American Korean Mexican drivers?

RANDY. I invited them. They didn't RSVP.

RICHARD. I don't even see them in the grandstands.

RANDY. You forgot the Transvestite Trobriand Islanders. They get pissy if you leave 'um out. Care for a Poppa's Popular Pork Rind?

RICHARD. No, thank you.

RANDY. What's wrong, scared of a piggy?

RICHARD. Give me those! I am not afraid of pork rinds, look at me, I can eat pork rinds, yum yum, but does that make this a sport?

RANDY. Why don't you go back to women's tennis at Well-Lessie, Dicky Doodle. Or sissified synchronized swimming. That'd suit you.

(**RICHARD** *hits him.*)

RANDY. *(staggering)* Thought you were against violence, Richey.

RICHARD. We'll be back after this brief word from our sponsors.

(**RANDY** *passes out.*)

SCENE TWENTY: Walk, Pussy

(**ROCKY** *in bandages head to toe, in a wheelchair. A* **NURSE** *wheels him onstage.*)

ROCKY. I don't want to go.

NURSE. Try.

ROCKY. I'm not going back.

NURSE. Wimp.

ROCKY. I'm not racing.

NURSE. Has-been.

ROCKY. Damn it, Flossie –

NURSE. I'm not Flossie –

ROCKY. I want to give up, will you let me give up?

NURSE. Walk, Pussy.

ROCKY. I can't.

NURSE. Loser.

(**NURSE** *exits. Ghost music plays as a white light illumi-nates* **FLOSSIE.**)

FLOSSIE. If you can't walk, then drive, Pussy.

ROCKY. Flossie?

FLOSSIE. Drive!

Vrrrrrrrrooooooooooooommmmmmmmm!

(**ROCKY** *reaches out for* **FLOSSIE. FLOSSIE** *pushes his chair off-stage like a race car.*)

SCENE TWENTY-ONE: Shell Game

(Karaoke bar: "THE THIRSTY MUSKRAT." The song "Muskrat Love" plays in the background. SLY and CHIP play the shell game. They're drinking together, having a damn good time. SLY moves the shells around. CHIP tries to guess which one has the peanut under it.)

CHIP. You da man.

SLY. No. You da man.

CHIP. No, you da man.

SLY. No, you are the man. Trust me on that.

> *(SLY stops the shells.*
>
> *He picks wrong again. SLY moves the shells around.)*

CHIP. I've got to ask you something. Seriously.

SLY. *(uneasy)* Okay...

> *(SLY stops the shells. CHIP picks wrong again. SLY shuffles the shells.)*

CHIP. If you were a cannibal...

SLY. A cannibal?

CHIP. No. wait. I got it wrong. If you were crashed on a desert island with one other guy and there was no food – would you eat him so that you could survive?

SLY. Eat him? Do I like him?

CHIP. He's your best friend.

SLY. Does he look tasty?

CHIP. He's one fat tasty son of a gun.

SLY. I don't know, would you eat him?

CHIP. Nope. I'd die.

SLY. Then he'd eat you.

  If it's eat or be eaten, I'd eat him.

CHIP. That's the difference between us. I'd die.

  What if it was me?

> *(CHIP stops SLY's hands.)*

Would you eat me?

SLY. Damn, you are a strange guy, you know that?

(**CHIP** *picks one. Wrong again.*)

SLY. Gotcha!

(**CHIP** *points to the shells.*)

CHIP. Is there really something under there?

(**SLY** *shuffles the shells again.*)

CHIP. Man, I like you! I get this feeling when I'm with you.

SLY. This is deja vu.

(**CHIP** *puts his hand on* **SLY**'s *hands, stopping the game.*)

CHIP. Look at me. I like you, now. I really like you.

SLY. Uh. I got to go to bed.

CHIP. Sly, there's something I got to know —

SLY. I like you too Chip. In fact I love you. What the hell do you want me to do about it?

CHIP. I found it in the trash.

This.

Out back of your trailer.

(*He holds up a shampoo bottle.*)

Cocamydopoopiedoll.

SLY. Shampoo?

CHIP. A fuel additive.

I gotta know.

SLY. Chip. Buddy —

CHIP. Did you mess with her car?

I'll believe you. Whatever you tell me.

SLY. It's late Chip. And you're drunk.

CHIP. I just got to know.

Because I love racing.

Didja do it?

(**SLY** *says nothing.*)

CHIP. I love this sport.

> Because no matter who you are
> I don't care if you drive for Walmart or Home Depot or
> Super Targay – I'm not – I mean Target.
> You got a fair chance at winning.
> We're all equal out there.
> It's all equal.
>
> Come on,
> Tell me you didn't
> And I'll toss this bottle
> Back in the trash
> We'll forget it.

SLY. Goodnight, Chip.

CHIP. What would you do? Sly, if you were me? Would you turn you in?

> (**SLY** *kisses him.*)

CHIP. Sly?

SLY. You're the cannibal.

CHIP. If you say you didn't, I'll believe you.

> (**SLY** *turns over the shells to reveal a nut under one.*)

SLY. Goodnight Chip.

> (**SLY** *exits.*)

CHIP. Shit.

> (*Transition to the raceway stands.*)

SCENE TWENTY-TWO: Aussie

*(**ROCKY** sits in the stands with a new guy watching race
practice. A driver we haven't seen before. This is **LEGS**
posing as a new driver – a man – **FLASH**. He has an
Australian accent.)*

LEGS/FLASH. And what do I see but a crocodile crawling
up through the floorboard, Mate, with his jaws wide
open, going right for my thigh. So I grab him round
the neck, like so, and use my feet to steer the car. And
while I've got his jaws of steel held shut, I happen to
glance in my rear view mirror and what do I see but a
Wallaby! Ready to wallop me! I won't go into details
about how, Mate, but I won that race by a mile. I mean,
kilometer.

ROCKY. See him go, that's my son.

LEGS/FLASH. Look at him go.

ROCKY. He can drive.

LEGS/FLASH. Yeah, he's alright.

ROCKY. You're gonna have to beat him. You think you can
do that?

LEGS/FLASH. Racing in Australia, Mate. There's nothing
harder.

ROCKY. So, you want me to believe that you're just a Good
Samaritan.

LEGS/FLASH. Paved track. Looks easy. What do you say,
Mate? How about you let ol' Flash give it a try.

ROCKY. You think you're gonna take my place?

LEGS/FLASH. Nah.

ROCKY. You think this is gonna help your career?

LEGS/FLASH. I just like the feeling.

ROCKY. You trying to edge me out here?

LEGS/FLASH. I like drivin' fast.

ROCKY. I'm gonna be back.

LEGS/FLASH. So, does that mean you're gonna let me drive
it?

ROCKY. Hmmm. What're you gonna do, Aussie, when your car goes up in smoke and you're trapped in an inferno out there?

LEGS/FLASH. I won't wreck your car –

ROCKY. You got any scars, Aussie?

LEGS/FLASH. You want to talk scars, Mate?

ROCKY. My ass looks like an alligator that's been barbecued on a hellfire grill by the devil himself.

LEGS/FLASH. Aw, that's nothing mate, my scull here, shattered into a 110 pieces and it took 50 surgeons to put it back together with Super Glue.

ROCKY. That's nothing, I got run over by Meals on Wheels. Still got the vanilla pudding in the crack of my ass.

LEGS/FLASH. Well, my uncle –

ROCKY. Oh, you want to talk family –

LEGS/FLASH. My uncle hit a kiwi fruit on the track once, and his car did 49 flips in the air before it came down, SMACK, made fruit salad of the whole pit crew.

ROCKY. My father died from a heart attack on the final lap of the Daytona 500, willed himself back to life and then got run over by the ambulance coming to save him.

LEGS/FLASH. That's nothing –

ROCKY. And he got up and drove the ambulance across the finish line. Won the race.

LEGS/FLASH. My grandmum was decapitated by a car hood.

ROCKY. That must've been a sad day.

LEGS/FLASH. Especially for Granddad, it was his favorite car.

ROCKY. And then, there's Flossie.

LEGS/FLASH. Oh. Flossie.

ROCKY. My wife, Flossie, got smacked in the head by a spoiler.

*(Pause. **FLASH** is silent.)*

Right here. On this spot.

And I miss her.

What's a matter, Aussie, can't beat that?

LEGS/FLASH. I'm sorry, Mate.

ROCKY. That was before fences. When you really took your chances coming to see a race.

LEGS/FLASH. We all take our chances, Mate. We gotta go on.

ROCKY. Yeah, but how?

LEGS. You find a way. You let me drive.

ROCKY. You got balls.

LEGS/FLASH. Well, you gonna let me or not?

ROCKY. Okay. Here's the thing, Aussie, rules say I gotta make it a lap, I'm the driver, that's all I gotta do to stay in. Then we switch out, you slide in the window, run the race for me. You win? I still get the points. You lose, we both look bad.

LEGS/FLASH. I won't disappoint.

(**LEGS/FLASH** *turns to go.*)

ROCKY. Hey, Flash.

LEGS/FLASH. Yeah?

ROCKY. Lousy accent.

You better work on that, Lady.

SCENE TWENTY-THREE: Friends

(**RICHARD** *and* **RANDY** *on the air. They are surprisingly agreeable.*)

RICHARD. So, on the eve of the big race... where do we stand, Randy?

RANDY. Richard, It's anybody's game, Richard, it's anybody's race, Richard.

RICHARD. It is, Randy, it's incredibly exciting, Bubba, why don't you recap for our television viewers?

RANDY. No, you recap, Richard, go ahead –

RICHARD. No, you.

RANDY. No, you, please, Richard, be my guest, Richard.

RICHARD. Well sure, Bubba. Let's see. It seems that Holly Legs Nelson was caught with an illegal substance -

RANDY. Shampoo.

RICHARD. Shampoo, Randy, yes, that's exactly right, in her catch can. Your instincts were right on the money!

RANDY. Thank you, Richard, how kind of you to say.

RICHARD. They then, done took away her car and banned her butt for the remainder of the season, but then Charlie Sly Fox was discovered to have done the dirty deed so his butt is banned for life and both have disappeared mysteriously from the public eye.

RANDY. Which makes you wonder, Richard.

RICHARD. It sure does, Randy. Meanwhile, the old veteran, Rocky Kane, is bandaged up like a mummy from head to toe and a strange Australian shows up on the scene as his replacement driver. And that's racing, Bubba!

RANDY. That's racing Richard!

RICHARD. What a terrific season!

RANDY.	**RICHARD.**
You know, Racing...	It seems, Racing...
RANDY.	**RICHARD.**
Go ahead.	Go ahead.

RANDY. No, you, Richard.

RICHARD. It seems, Racing… Randy, are you thinking what I'm thinking?

RICHARD & RANDY. Racing, brings out the best in people.

RANDY. It sure does, Richard. The best.

RICHARD. Care for a pork rind?

SCENE TWENTY-FOUR:
Who dunnit? In the Karaoke Bar

(The Karaoke bar sign reads: "THE THIRSTY ROAD-KILL." THE MAN IN THE HAT *enters.)*

MAN IN THE HAT. I've been busier than a cat covering crap on a marble floor.

Give me a Coors light.

*(***WENDY/SLY*** *enters and sits.* **CHIP** *enters from another direction.)*

CHIP. Has anybody seen Sly?

WAITRESS. He pulled outta town last night –

MAN IN THE HAT. Good riddance. A Coors light, Sweetie.

CHIP. I need to talk to him – explain –

(He sees Wendy.)

Hi.

WENDY/SLY. Explain what?

CHIP. I'm Chip Chowalsky.

WENDY/SLY. Aren't you the one who ratted him out?

MAN IN THE HAT. Brought him to NASCAR justice. Cleaned this sport up!

WENDY/SLY. Nudged him out so you could get ahead tomorrow?

WAITRESS. If you ask me –

MAN IN THE HAT. Nobody asked, Sweetie. Now about that Coors Light. With a smile.

*(***THE WAITRESS*** *exits.* **FLASH** *enters.)*

CHIP. Hi, I'm Chip, did I say that? You are?

MAN IN THE HAT. Wendy! Everybody, this is Wendy, wha wha wha Wendy!

CHIP. Wendy?

WENDY/SLY. Wendy.

CHIP. Wendy.

WENDY/SLY. Wendy.

CHIP. Wendy. Do you believe in love at first sight?

> (**LEGS/FLASH** *examines* **WENDY/SLY**. *They recognize each other.*)

LEGS/FLASH. New Lady Driver, ay?

WENDY/SLY. Do I know you?

LEGS/FLASH. You wouldn't. I'm from Australia. Flash.

MAN IN THE HAT. Flash is stepping in for Rocky tomorrow.

WENDY/SLY. Australia huh? How interesting. What part of Australia?

LEGS/FLASH. Dingo. Dingo, Australia.

WENDY/SLY. I know Australia like the back of my hand. Never heard of Dingo.

MAN IN THE HAT. Wendy is replacing Sly.

LEGS/FLASH. Replacing Sly why?

MAN IN THE HAT. Chip caught that Sly fox red-handed.

LEGS/FLASH. Doing what?

MAN IN THE HAT. Sabotaging Holly Legs Nelson's Chevy!

LEGS/FLASH. Really! You mean Holly Nelson didn't cheat?

MAN IN THE HAT. Nah, but the trouble is, we can't find her, she's gone A.W.O.L. And if you ask me we're better off without her. Women, huh?

LEGS/FLASH. Yeah, women. More trouble than they're worth.

MAN IN THE HAT. Rest assured, Racers, you're safe as a curled up kitten out there tomorrow. There ain't no saboteur on the loose, among us.

LEGS/FLASH. So, Sly has been brought to justice?

WENDY/SLY. Oh my purse! Must've left it in the ladies room.

CHIP. Wait! I've got a song for you! Do you like The Carpenters?

> (**WENDY/SLY** *exits.* **CHIP** *follows.*)

MAN IN THE HAT. Dingo, now, is that on the coast?

LEGS/FLASH. Be right back, Mate –

(LEGS/FLASH exits. ROCKY enters. He's wearing new "BEAN-O" sponsor attire.)

MAN IN THE HAT. Like your new sponsor.

(He makes a farting sound.)

Bean-o.

(He farts again.)

I could use some of that.

ROCKY. Where's Flash?

MAN IN THE HAT. Where's that waitress with my damn Coors Light is the question.

ROCKY. Tell him I'm sorry, but I'm racing tomorrow.

MAN IN THE HAT. You're racing?

ROCKY. He's out, I'm in. Tell him.

MAN IN THE HAT. But you're a mess.

ROCKY. I'm gettin' my car together, and I'm gonna win this thing myself.

MAN IN THE HAT. Why are you dong this to yourself, Rock?

ROCKY. For Flossie. Gotta win one more for Flossie.

MAN IN THE HAT. I hate to tell ya. But I always thought that woman never was no good for you.

*(FLOSSIE appears and starts walking toward the **MAN IN THE HAT**. **ROCKY** sees **FLOSSIE** and signals to the **MAN IN THE HAT** to stop.)*

MAN IN THE HAT. She drove you crazy. She was a terrible mother, couldn't cook for shit. And sure hope you didn't have any lights in your bedroom, cuz that woman was butt ugly.

(FLOSSIE smacks him.)

MAN IN THE HAT. What the heck was that?

FLOSSIE. *(to **ROCKY**)* DRIVE, PUSSY!

*(ROCKY exits. **FLOSSIE** hits **MAN IN THE HAT** again and exits.)*

MAN IN THE HAT. Damn. What was in that chimichanga?

(CHIP enters.)

CHIP. She went into the restroom and I lost her. You think she's coming out? Wendy?

MAN IN THE HAT. She's outta your league, Chowalsky.

CHIP. What is it about me?

MAN IN THE HAT. *(sudden realization)* Whoa! I've got to make a pit stop.

(**THE MAN IN THE HAT** *exits.* **CHIP** *picks up the karaoke microphone.*)

CHIP. Number 4, Sylvia.

(**CHIP** *sings Karaoke, a few lines from a sentimental tune like The Carpenters' "Close to You."* **WENDY/SLY** *enters. He senses she is near.* **CHIP** *sings to her.* **WENDY** *moves toward* **CHIP** *in slow motion, then the music cuts out, she leans over and picks up her purse instead.*)

WENDY/SLY. Oh, there's my purse. Found it.

(**WENDY/SLY** *exits.*)

CHIP. Wait! Wendy!

(**CHIP** *exits.* **THE WAITRESS** *enters.*)

WAITRESS. Coors light?

(Instantly realizes the Man in the Hat is gone.)

Asshole.

(*The* **WAITRESS** *exits.* **WENDY/SLY** *enters with* **LEGS/FLASH** *in hot pursuit. Whispering.*)

LEGS/FLASH. Give me one good reason not to blow your cover!

WENDY/SLY. Because I'll blow yours!

LEGS/FLASH. You sabotaged my car, Bitch, I'm off the hook.

WENDY/SLY. It wasn't me, Bitch.

LEGS/FLASH. The hell it wasn't, Bitch.

WENDY/SLY. I was framed. You've got to help me clear my name.

LEGS/FLASH. I don't need your help.

WENDY/SLY. Why? Because you're the L'eggs Pantyhose Heiress, Bitch –

LEGS/FLASH. That's no reason to sabotage me, Bitch!

WENDY/SLY. Look, Bitch, whoever it was is still out here on the loose and ready to strike again!

LEGS/FLASH. If you didn't do it, then who did?

(**HOTSHOT** *enters. They watch him.*)

WENDY/SLY. Who do you think?

LEGS/FLASH. Hotshot?

WENDY/SLY. He took both of us out with one move.

LEGS/FLASH. You think?

WENDY/SLY. There's only one way to find out.

(**LEGS/FLASH** *and* **WENDY/SLY** *approach* **HOTSHOT.**)

LEGS/FLASH. G'day mate –

WENDY/SLY. Hello, handsome.

You're looking awfully thoughtful –

LEGS/FLASH. Got something on your mind?

HOTSHOT. Legs Nelson.

LEGS/FLASH. Did her wrong, eh?

WENDY/SLY. How'd you do it?

HOTSHOT. What are you talking about?

LEGS/FLASH. Sabotage her car?

WENDY/SLY. Cut yourself a clear path to Victory Lane?

HOTSHOT. You want to take this outside?

LEGS/FLASH. Right here, Mate!

WENDY/SLY. *(to* **LEGS***)* What are you doing?

LEGS/FLASH. *(to* **SLY***)* I'm gonna kick his ass.

WENDY/SLY. Are you crazy?

LEGS/FLASH. Choose your weapon!

WENDY/SLY. I'm going for help.

(**WENDY/SLY** *exits.*)

HOTSHOT. Bare hands.

LEGS/FLASH. Street rules.

HOTSHOT. Wrestling.

LEGS/FLASH. Greco-Roman.

HOTSHOT. Numchucks.

LEGS/FLASH. Ninja.

HOTSHOT. Karaoke.

LEGS/FLASH. Anything goes.

(A Karaoke tune cuts in – something Heavy Metal with a loud screaming start. **LEGS/FLASH** *wails – but* **HOTSHOT** *interrupts.)*

HOTSHOT. Wait a minute, this is all wrong. Wrong song. Because Anger is just fear. And I realize now that what I'm afraid of is sweet sweet love.

(Music changes to something sappy and sweet like "What the World Needs Now is Love Sweet Love," underscoring the following speech.)

I'm gonna send this one out to Holly Legs Nelson. Wherever you are. Holly, I'm sorry, Baby. I let these little things get in the way of loving you.

So what if you won nearly every race of the season and made me look bad. What's it matter?

So what if my daddy was bleeding to death on the track and you were busting my balls for something I didn't do. I shouldn't let that affect how I feel about you.

You were never the problem, Baby, it was never you. It was me. I'm sorry.

You had me at "Hello."

And I want you back.

*(***LEGS/FLASH*** *walks over and gives him a hug.* **JOANY** *enters, sees the two "men" in an embrace.)*

JOANY. I'm sorry, is this a bad time?

HOTSHOT. Thanks, Man, I needed that.

*(***HOTSHOT*** *pats* **FLASH** *on the butt. Exits.)*

JOANY. I'm sorry, have you seen Holly Legs Nelson?

LEGS/FLASH. Depends on who's asking.

JOANY. It's me, Joany, from Chicago. I need to talk to her. It was me, I did it, I put the Cocomydropapoopinall in her catch can. I feel awful, but I just had to make sure she won. For me. For women everywhere!

LEGS/FLASH. I remember you.

(*MITCHIE enters. He walks to the middle of the room and puts down a bottle of shampoo.*)

MITCHIE. WITH A REBEL YELL I CRIED –
I did it! I stalked Legs Nelson. Sabotage is a rush. It's righteous!

JOANY. Mitchie –

MITCHIE. Mom, You don't have to lie for me. I put the cocopuffandstuff in her catch can!

(*CASSIE runs in.*)

CASSIE. LIAR LIAR PANTS ON FIRE! You suck you copycat freak.

JOANY. Cassie!

MITCHIE. Death.

JOANY. Mitchie!

MITCHIE. Die!

CASSIE. He soooooooooo didn't do it. Because I totally did! I put the cocomydamachiado-aol in her catch can!

(*MITCHIE exits. CASSIE exits.*)

JOANY. Cassie honey, you didn't. She didn't do it.

(*JOANY exits. The WAITRESS enters.*)

WAITRESS. Damn right she didn't do it. They think I'm just a waitress, but they have misunderestimated me.

(*She reaches down her shirt, and pulls hotel size shampoo bottle from her brassiere.*)

All my life I've been called a Nobody. But I am a SOMEBODY! I am a SABOTEUR!

I put the Cocomydadroppalapadingdong in Legs Nelson's gas tank, people! I did it! Slap the cuffs on me and put me on Oprah!

LEGS. I need a drink.

WAITRESS. Get it yourself, Honey. I quit!

> (*The* **WAITRESS** *exits.* **CHICKEN 2** *enters, stepping out of the shadows with a gun.*)

CHICKEN 2. Who's seen Legs Nelson? You? She cost me and the Clucker a whole lotta dough. So if ya happen to see Legs, tell her she's got to come over to the Chicken's side of the road before we flatten her like a pancake. You look awful familiar.

> (**THE MAN IN THE HAT** *enters dressed in a robe or towel, his hair lathered with shampoo.* **CHICKEN 2** *hides the gun.*)

MAN IN THE HAT. *(to audience)* Don't listen to these people, people. Cause I did it. I put the cocomochalabradoodle in her catch can.

I just couldn't bear to see a girl win. Goddamn it, it's not American.

You all woulda done the same thing! Racing is business! Heck, I got a guilty conscience. I can't even get shampoo'd without feeling dirty.

> (*The* **INSPECTOR** *enters [also in a towel?] with a lather on his hands and a bottle of shampoo.*)

INSPECTOR. And I can't shampoo you without feeling dirty. I did it! I put the cocalakaloolooloo in Legs Nelson's engyna!

LEGS/FLASH. ENOUGH! I don't care who did it.

> (**LEGS** *takes off her* **FLASH** *disguise – revealing she is* **LEGS NELSON.***)

ALL. Legs!

LEGS. The point is. Someone's going to win the cup tomorrow morning. Someone is going to Victory Lane. One person.

> (**CHIP** *enters. Everybody looks at him.*)

CHIP. What'd I miss?

(The door to the theater opens and **RICHARD PETTY** *drives in on a motorcycle. He is the king of racing.)*

ALL. Richard Petty!

RICHARD PETTY. Yup.

I've been listening to you boys and ladies and I've had about enough of your whining.

I believe you've lost something racers

And I'm here to help you find it.

What are you looking at, Chicken?

*(***CHICKEN 2*** *clucks)*

Got a problem?

CHICKEN 2. Nothing – no, not me.

ELVIS. Well, I've got a big problem with you. You're what's wrong with this sport.

(He addresses **THE INSPECTOR**.*)*

And you, not so fast, cheating's American as your mama's apple pie, it's what we do.

(He grabs **THE MAN IN THE HAT**, *who is trying to sneak away.)*

And you, where do you think you're goin', you think you're the king of racing, but there are only three kings in racing. Me, Jesus H Christ and Elvis Aaron Presley.

Now I could stand here all day giving you a sermon.

But I think these folks would rather see a race.

Suit up, Gentlemen. And ladies.

Get your racing gear on.

(As **RICHARD PETTY** *speaks, the racers strip off their other costumes to reveal their race clothes. They suit up onstage, getting ready to race.)*

Get outta of that chicken suit, get out of that stupid costume.

Lets get racing.

I'm taking you back to basics. Back to square one.

(He rips the logos off their uniforms as he talks to the audience.)

RICHARD PETTY. Gone is Colonel Cluckers Chicken, gone
is Boo-Hoos Butt Paste, and Nextel and Pentel and
Pentax, Xerox, Zantax and Tampax. All gone. The TV
cameras gone. The new supersized superslick super-
speedway, gone. The new and improved rules gone.
Gone, gone.
Instead.
It's Saturday night
At the race track
The Ford flathead V-8's are firing up
You can smell the gasoline
You're drivin' on sand.
Across a Florida beach.
Sliding full-throttle into the turns
Sand Flying
Balls out, belly to the ground
You're drivin cuz your Daddy drove.
You're drivin cuz the faster you go, the freer you feel
You're drivin to run moonshine across the state line.
You're drivin cuz it feels good to press the pedal to the
floorboard
You're driving cuz it feels damn good to speed.
You're competing to compete.
You're racing to race.
You're cheating to win.
It's pure.
Simple.

ALL. Amen!

RICHARD PETTY. Now, who wants to see a race?
I said, who wants to see a race?

(The crowd cheers. The racers line up. Ready to go.)

ROCKY. Good luck, Son.

HOTSHOT. Same to you, Dad.

SLY. May the best woman win.

LEGS. You're looking good, Hotshot.

HOTSHOT. Drive the wheels off it, Lady.

CHIP. Please, God, just let me finish.

ALL. SEE YOU IN VICTORY LANE.

RICHARD PETTY. Ladies and Gentlemen, Start your engines.

(**RICHARD PETTY** *cues the sound operator to start the music. He dances to famous racing songs. He controls the starting and stopping of the music as they play a vicious game of musical chairs. A different song is used for each round. When the music stops, the racers scramble for chairs. The outcome should be different every night. A real competition. After each round, a chair is removed. When a racer is caught out [with no chair] she turns to the audience and delivers her epilogue. The contest is repeated until one winner sits, victorious. As the final two epilogues are delivered, music builds underneath until, at the conclusion of the winner's epilogue,* **RICHARD PETTY** *screams over the music: "Ladies and Gentlemen, we have a winner!" Champagne explodes, milk flows, everyone gets drenched in wild celebration.*)

The **RACERS** *epilogues:*

CHIP CHOWALSKY races three more years before retiring in Utah, where he marries 3 women in a polygamous ceremony. Immediately following the honeymoon, he ends up with ex-wives 5, 6, and 7. But don't worry, Chip's luck finally takes a turn for the better when he records and releases his hit country album, "Fuckin' Chicken," and runs into Wha Wha Wha Wendy Albertson in a grocery store. Together, they open up a pet shop. Breeding prize hairless Chihuahuas. And I finally finish first. In the Westminster Dog Show.

WENDY aka CHARLIE SLY FOX, this year's Rookie of the Year, gets suspended next year for some "dirty dealings." But don't worry, she gets back on track and realizes that racing is just a horrible addiction and becomes a spokeswoman for Nascarholics Anonymous and an editor of the annual Automobile Burn Victims Cookbook. Chip Chowalski stalks me until I finally take him in as a "charity case" along with his prize dogs. Fucking Chihuahuas.

HOLLY LEGS NELSON writes her memoir, *My Winning Year: A Girls Guide to NASCAR Victory,* and is banned from racing for the rest of the decade. She and Hotshot eventually give in and get married during a race (his idea of course), and have one child who they hope never goes into racing. Eventually they separate (her fault), and after a brief bout of sadness, I move on with my life.

ROCKY KANE threatens to retire every year but continues racing to this day. Has moved through a series of sponsors including but not limited to: Elmer's Glue, Rogaine, Jumbo Huggies and Sunsweet Prunes. In his spare time he finally enjoys extreme Paraskiing, Alpine peak jumping, and long walks on the beach. In the raceway stands where my wife died, I erect a memorial. A chrome plated spoiler and Pontiac hood.

KENNY "HOTSHOT" KANE THE THIRD gets down on his knee in the grandstand and proposes to Holly Legs Nelson shortly after this race. They get married on treacherous turn 4 of the Talladega Superspeedway (her idea of course). They name their first child Kenny Kane the 4th in hopes that he'll go into racing. Later, they separate (his fault), and are in the process of getting back together. He gets promoted from Racer of the Year to middle management. I dream of better things for my son.

End of Play

COSTUMES

The actors can remain in their racing-suits throughout the entire show and costume pieces can be added over or under the race-suits for character changes. Hats, sunglasses, wigs, etc. are effective ways of defining a new character while allowing for a quick transformation. Here are some suggestions for costumes.

Actor # 1

Chip: Green racing suit with sponsor logos, sunglasses and a NASCAR cap.
Randy: A suit coat. Good Ol' boy style.
Joany: A NASCAR race shirt and a sun hat.

Actor # 2

Legs: Pink racing suit with sponsor logos, sunglasses and a NASCAR cap.
Flossie: A big black sun hat and veil. A black dress and gloves.
Flip: Race fan shirt with cutoff sleeves.
Flash: A black racing suit with Australian logos, sunglasses, a NASCAR cap.

Actor # 3

Sly: Blue racing suit with sponsor logos, mirrored sunglasses, a mustache, a NASCAR cap.
Richard: A suit coat. Very conservative.
Chicken 2: Same chicken suit as chicken 1.
Mitchie: A black trench coat.
Wendy: Wearing Sly's racing suit. Long hair.

Actor # 4

Rocky: Yellow racing suit with sponsor logos, sunglasses, a NASCAR cap.
Waitress: Apron and waitress top or sexy shirt.
Inspector: A white lab coat. Glasses.

Actor # 5

Hotshot: Red racing suit with sponsor logos, sunglasses, a NASCAR cap.
Chicken 1: A chicken suit.
Man in The Hat: An enormous white cowboy hat.
Cassie: A tube top
Nurse: A white nurses uniform and red cross nurse's hat.

Actor # 6

Richard Petty: Richard Petty style hat, mustache, western shirt and jeans.
Naked Fan: Naked. Or wearing red white and blue bikini bottoms.
Shadowy Figure: All black clothes and hood like a cat burglar.
Grandma: A flowered housedress.

PROPS

Scene 1
Steering wheels for racers to hold
    while driving
Announcer's headsets or
    microphones

Scene 2
Beer cans
Towels

Scene 3
Announcer's headsets or
    microphones

Scene 4
A trash can
A slinky
A hotdog
Announcer's headsets or
    microphones

Scene 5
A sign that reads "The Thirsty Worm"
Microphone
Beer cans
Money

Scene 6
A bucket of chicken
One piece of chicken

Scene 7
A sign that reads "The Thirsty
    Armadillo"
Beer cans
Darts
Money
Wallet

Scene 8
House of cards
Waitress tray
2 cocktail glasses

Scene 9
Racing helmet

Scene 10
Announcer's headsets or
    microphones
Whoopee cushion

Scene 11
Plastic Tarp
Nail polish
Toolbox or wheeling tool caddy
    containing:
Plastic gloves
Measuring tape
Magnifying glass
Dental floss
Chewing gum
Hair dryer
Tweezers

Scene 12
Announcer's headsets or
    microphones
Enormous cooler
2 transistor radios
Race flags
Beer cans
Pair of pantyhose
Grandma's cane
Joany's purse
A lighter
L'eggs pantyhose egg

Scene 13
A contract

Scene 14
Sly's mustache

Scene 15
Announcer's headsets or
    microphones
Racer's steering wheels

Scene 16
Plastic tarp
Toolbox or wheeling tool caddy
A tiny scale
A strange looking metal piece
A test tube with a strange yellow
    liquid

Scene 18
Sign that reads "The Thirsty Fruitfly"
Darts
Waitress tray
Beer cans
Microphone

Scene 19
Announcer's headsets or microphones
Bag of pork rinds

Scene 20
Bandages
Wheelchair

Scene 21
A sign that reads "The Thirsty Muskrat"
4 walnut shells
A peanut
A shampoo bottle

Scene 22
Bandages

Scene 23
Announcer's headsets or microphones
Bag of pork rinds

Scene 24
A sign that reads "The Thirsty Road-kill"
Beer cans
Waitress tray
Wendy's purse
Microphone
3 bottles of shampoo
A hotel size bottle of shampoo
A gun
A towel or robe
A motorcycle
Champagne

SCENIC DESIGN

Set Pieces:

Bleachers or bench
Racecar
Bar/Locker rolling unit
Locker room bench
Trash can
2 Bar tables
2 Bar stools
5 rolling chairs
2-3 clothing racks
Television studio platform (with possible rear projection)
Cyc or backdrop

* TABLES + BAR ON CASTERS

TABLE

TABLE

B
A
R

5 CHAIRS ON CASTERS

Basic groundplan. 4ff. "VROOOMMM".